STAMPEDE

Jeb was a single-minded man. He came out West to discover who had bushwhacked his brother, and he had no interest in running the small ranch that was left. He wasn't concerned about who ran the other small ranches around either, or whether the nesters could be scared off the land claimed by the empire.

But when Jeb was strung up by the thumbs, he discovered right quick whose side he was on. And suddenly it became even more urgent to find out who had killed Tom—for all Jeb knew, he might be siding with his brother's murderer.

Chad Merriman was the pseudonym Giff Cheshire used for his first novel, *Blood on the Sun*, published by Fawcett Gold Medal in 1952. He was born in 1905 on a homestead in Cheshire, Oregon. The county was named for his grandfather who had crossed the plains in 1852 by wagon from Tennessee, and the homestead was the same one his grandfather had claimed upon his arrival. Cheshire's early life was colored by the atmosphere of the Old West which in the first decade of the century had not yet been modified by the automobile. He attended public schools in Junction City and, following high school, enlisted in the U.S. Marine Corps and saw duty in Central America. In 1929 he came to the Portland area in Oregon and from 1929 to 1943 worked for the U.S. Corps of Engineers. By 1944, after moving to Beaverton, Oregon, he found he could make a living writing Western and North-Western short fiction for the magazine market, and presently stories under the byline Giff Cheshire began appearing in *Lariat Story Magazine*, *Dime Western*, and *North-West Romances*. His short story *Strangers in the Evening* won the Zane Grey Award in 1949. Cheshire's Western fiction was characterized from the beginning by a wider historical panorama of the frontier than just cattle ranching and frequently the settings for his later novels are in his native Oregon. *Thunder on the Mountain* (1960) focuses on Chief Joseph and the Nez Perce War, while *Wenatchee Bend* (1966) and *A Mighty Big River* (1967) are among his best-known titles. However, his Chad Merriman novels for Fawcett Gold Medal remain among his most popular works, notable for their complex characters, expert pacing, and authentic backgrounds.

STAMPEDE

Chad Merriman

GUNSMOKE

First published in the UK by Transworld

This hardback edition 2005
by BBC Audiobooks Ltd
by arrangement with
Golden West Literary Agency

ISBN 1 4056 8034 2

British Library Cataloguing in Publication Data available.

Printed and bound in Great Britain by
Antony Rowe Ltd., Chippenham, Wiltshire

Chapter 1

THE EARTH was fresh and covered with rocks, concealed here under the leafless cottonwoods. Beyond the mount, sagebrush swayed to the bluff edge of Dogleg Mountain. Southward, the Sapphires pushed toward the chilly fall sky and the dismalness seeped into him as he looked at the iron-burned letters on the new pine headboard.

Jeb stepped down from the saddle and walked forward, stiff from the cold long ride from the railroad. A breeze stirred the black branches of the trees and their rasping lost itself in the tumbling complaint of Battle Creek. He pulled off his hat but his instinctive reverence was swept away in an abrupt explosion of anger.

Somebody had added a line to the lettering on the headboard, using a pencil. Closer up, it read:

HERE LIES
TOM PELTON
A DIRTY NESTER

Cash Donovan kneed his horse closer, saying sharply, "What's wrong?" His eyes swept toward the grave and there was no need to answer him. After a moment he said, "Well, I pegged them a notch above desecratin' a grave. I was wrong, I guess."

"When were you here last?" Jeb Pelton said.

"Yesterday. Somebody done it while I was in town to meet you." Cash had sent the wire that brought Jeb here to the heart of Nevada's cattle country. He swung down and started to rip up the headboard with a furious jerk. Jeb stopped him.

"Leave it be. I'll get the man responsible for that and let him clean it off." He walked to his horse. When Cash started to follow suit, he stopped him again. "I reckon this is something I'll handle alone. He was your partner but my brother."

"Sure," Cash said. "You'll find him on Dollarmark."

"That goes without sayin'."

The big outfit's headquarters stood in the angle formed by Sperling Creek and its south fork. Jeb cut the creek road and swung west and in about an hour reached his destination. The crew was nooning when he rode into the sprawling yard. The corral was full of horses brought in for the afternoon's mount and riders loitered about or washed up outside the bunkhouse door. Over to the left stood the big log ranchhouse, with no one in evidence outdoors.

Jeb was unknown here but the punchers recognized the horse Cash had brought to town for him to ride out. They inspected him in uneasy curiosity when, wholly silent, he reined in. They saw a high, wide-chested man whose weather-stained face reflected the deadly glint of his eyes.

"I want the son," Jeb said, "that used a pencil on Tom Pelton's headboard."

That was news to some, maybe to all of them. Every man there looked at somebody else for a glimmer of understanding, their hostility shooting up like steam from a valve. Some of them were armed and all were aggressive instantly.

"Who're you?" a big, black-faced man said roughly.

"Jeb Pelton."

"The hombre Tom liked to brag about, eh? The fastest gun west of the Rockies."

"If I am it'll come in handy when I get the man who bushwhacked him. That can keep. Right now I want the joker who marked up his grave."

"I don't know what you're talkin' about."

"Here comes Hock," a man cut in. "Better let him handle it, Lot."

A horse had shoved up from the creek ford off to the left. Its rider, Jeb saw, was Hock Sperling himself, a gaunt, grey man who even in the saddle showed the arrogance the cattle barons often developed. Sperling rode up to them, recognizing trouble without understanding it yet. His eyes were frosty and a pair of mustaches hung past the ends of a merciless mouth.

"This here's Jeb Pelton," the man called Lot said angrily. "Seems to be exercised over somethin' he claims we done to his brother's grave. Sort of hinted we killed him, too."

Sperling's seamy features assumed the truculence of the men. "What's in your craw, Pelton?" he said, his voice flat and harsh.

"You heard him."

Sperling made an irritated motion with his bony hand, shaking his head in dismissal. "I supposed that lyin' bunch of nesters would claim we killed Tom Pelton. It ain't hard to see why. They're trying to justify their squattin' on my land. My men never filled his grave, Pelton. If somebody's done somethin' else to it, we don't know a thing about it."

Jeb came close to living up to his brother's boast about him. A gun appeared in his hand and lined on Sperling's chest before the watchers knew what was happening.

"You're responsible, Sperling, so I reckon you'll do. The rest of you stay put or he's dead. Except you, there. Empty that water pail and hand it to him."

He heard a growl pass from throat to throat and knew he was on the edge of disaster. Sperling stabilized his men momentarily by muttering, "Better do what he says." A puncher emptied the water bucket that had been on the bench. He handed it up to Sperling. They were all off balance for the moment, bewildered but ready to blow the place up.

"Don't anybody follow unless he wants to sing at this old turkey's funeral." Jeb began to back his horse, motioning Sperling to follow. "Better endorse that, too, old man."

"He's loco," Sperling said. "Stay out of it."

The crew watched with unhappy eyes but stood fixed. Cut off by the end of the cookshack, Jeb closed in and jerked Sperling's gun from its holster. Then he drove the old man ahead of him, riding fast. Dollarmark had accepted the situation momentarily but that wouldn't hold very long.

7

"Dunno what you're up to!" Sperling said explosively. "But you'll regret this!"

"Don't look for that right away, mister."

Jeb kept up the hard riding, rounding the end of the hump that divided Sperling Basin from the nester country. He didn't call a halt until they came down on Battle Creek. "Light down and fill that pail," he said curtly. "Half water and the rest sand. Quick about it."

Sperling looked at him, obviously puzzled, saw death in the eyes watching him, and cursed under his breath. He swung down and followed orders. Jeb told him to remount and forced him to go on to Tom's grave in the cottonwood stand. He pointed at the pencil-scrawled headboard.

"Start scrubbin'."

Sperling took a look at the grave and his eyes flashed. "If you think I'd let a man do a thing like that—"

"You heard what I said. Get busy."

"Be durned if I will."

The gun exploded in Jeb's hand. The cattleman's hat whipped off his head and tumbled to the ground. "The next'll be between the eyes, mister."

His grey face paler, Sperling swung down and carried his heavy pail to the grave. Jeb compelled him to use his bandana and scrub with sand and water until the defamation was obliterated. Then he handed back Sperling's gun.

"If you feel like using it, make your try."

"I feel like using it," Sperling said bitterly, but he jammed the piece in the holster. He picked up his hat and stared angrily at the bullet puncture. "You made a big mistake, Pelton. A man can understand you gettin' riled, but you sure brought your complaint to the wrong place." He walked to his horse, swung up with the nimbleness of a much younger man and headed south.

Cash Donovan stepped out of the brush. Jeb realized he had watched the proceedings, tactfully staying out of sight until Sperling had left. His earlier rancor had changed to gratification. "That was worth seeing—the old boy himself makin' amends. You mean to say you rode into Dollarmark and snaked him out from under

8

the noses of that big tough crew?" He chuckled. "Tom always claimed you were a ring-tailed snorter."

"I never fancied myself as one."

Cash gave him a sharp look, realizing the dangerous tensions still running high in him. Sobering, he said, "Well, I was fixin' a bait of grub when I seen you ride in with him. Let's go eat it."

They repaired to their headquarters—not much of a layout compared to Dollarmark, Jeb reflected. A one-room shack stood by Battle Creek and a low-roofed stable and a few corrals completed the setup. Trees surrounded the buildings and scabs of lava rock broke up the openness. The brand Tom and Cash had registered was a PD connected. The herd tallied only a few hundred head that ranged down the creek to the fenced railroad land Sperling owned, and east to Dogleg Mountain which he claimed along with the intervening range.

The land on this side of the Battle Creek divide was a slow-falling plateau that extended to the Humboldt. Where Sperling Basin was drained by a creek with several affluents, the plateau was cut by three streams flowing independently into the Humboldt. There was a nester outfit on each of them, Jeb knew. East of the Sapphires and connected to Sperling Basin by a broad gap was the second stretch of disputed rangeland, a section called Muleshoe Mesa where three more nesters had set themselves up as loners in the cattle business.

Violence had been building here quite a while, Jeb knew. Hock Sperling had once run cattle on both sections, as well as in the basin, until two successive hard winters had nearly wiped him out. The nesters had moved in while he was unable to range the entire area because his herds had been so drastically reduced. Now he was on his feet again and meant to regain what he still looked upon as his own.

Tom's death had been the first bloodshed. He had been shot out of the saddle while by himself on the range. Since it was raining hard at the time, the sign had washed out before the sheriff even got on the scene.

The wire from Cash had brought Jeb on the double, determined to take up where the law officer had left off. He still hadn't decided what to do about Tom's interest in the little P-D, however. He had ridden shotgun out of Randsburg, a roistering mining camp on the Mojave desert, longer than Tom had been here. He had intended to go back to it when he had settled other matters, but now he wondered if that would be as quick and easy as he had hoped. He had just thrown a lot of oil on a fire already burning briskly. He still didn't know just who had waylaid Tom, and things could get a lot worse here before he found out for sure.

They had finished eating when horses came down Battle Creek at a clatter. The two men in the shack sprang to their feet. Cash turned back from the window a breath later with a worried expression on his face, wiping away the youth that showed when he was more relaxed.

"Trouble. I think it's Dollarmark." He lunged to the corner of the room and swept up a rifle. He wasn't a large man but his body had power, and his motion was smoothly efficient. Jeb had already pegged him as a good man in a fight, but this particular business was not of his making.

"I'll see what they want," Jeb said, and started for the door.

"Not much," Cash said sharply. "You'll keep a wall in front of you till we know what they're up to."

That was prudent, and Jeb halted. The outside sounds broke off before the riders reached the house.

"You taught 'em a little respect," Cash muttered. "They don't exactly care to show themselves, either."

A shout punched across the distance. "Come outta there, Pelton, and be quick about it!"

"Who's that?" Jeb asked Cash.

"Sperling's ramrod, Lot Yerington." Jeb remembered him as the blank-faced big fellow who had done part of the talking at Dollarmark. Cash lifted his voice to a defiant yell. "If you want him come and get him!"

The answer was a storm of bullets that rattled against the house. Glass exploded in the window frame and the upper panel of the door. Cash thrust the rifle barrel through the window opening and whacked a bullet across the yard. Jeb remembered all the cover out there, trees and huge rocks. The walls of the unceiled shack were

10

much too thin to withstand the kind of siege that could be laid down. A second volley crashed out to emphasize that fact. Lead hit the stove and shrieked across the room. Nobody could live in that very long, and they both knew it.

"Hold your fire, Yerington!" Jeb yelled. "I'm coming out!"

"What for?" Cash said with an angry glare.

"I started this, and it's not your funeral."

"It'll be yours if I don't help you."

Bullets kept splintering the boards. "Yerington, lay off!" Jeb shouted. "I'm coming onto the porch!"

The guns went silent finally, and Cash cursed bitterly. "Man, they'll hang you. And if you don't want to fight it out, I'm goin' out there with you."

"Your way we're both done for," Jeb snapped. "My way we've got a chance. Stay here."

He went through the door to find that Dollarmark had dismounted up the creek and closed in on foot. There wasn't a man or horse in sight. He could hear the creek in the silence that was quickly broken by another call from out there.

"Toss the hogleg into the yard, Pelton!" The voice was still Yerington's. Jeb obeyed. "Now walk over here."

They were taking no chances with Cash and his rifle. Jeb settled for that and stepped off the porch, walking toward the voice that commanded him. He rounded a rock slab and two men stood behind it, both covering him. He placed Lot Yerington, whose face wore a look of brutal vengeance.

Jeb said, "Donovan's got no part in this particular squabble, Yerington. Leave him out of it."

"You're the boy we want now," Yerington said gustily. He lifted his voice. "Come in, you fellows. We got him."

In a moment half a dozen men had filtered to them through the heavy cover. They were all punchers he had seen at the Dollarmark bunkhouse. Wrath still twisted their faces but Jeb noticed that it was all centered on him for the time being. He settled for that, too, momentarily.

Yerington nodded up the creek and said, "Get going."

Chapter 2

FOR THE SECOND TIME that day Jeb Pelton rode into Dollarmark's yard. Eight armed and turbulent riders surrounded him. He had been little comforted that on the ride from Battle Creek they had not molested him. The punishment, whatever it was to be, would come here at Hock Sperling's seat of baronial power. His escort trotted toward a small building between the ranchhouse and other structures. This, he saw, was the business office. Sperling came to the door and laid his stony stare on the group, saying nothing.

"Here he is," Yerington said with ill-concealed triumph.

Still framed in the doorway, Sperling seemed entirely devoid of feeling. The impression was deceptive, Jeb knew. Pride rode a man of his nature with sharpened spurs, and with it was the pitiless hard-headedness such a pride demanded. No one could dispute that men like him had opened the West. The trouble was that some of them, like Sperling, granted themselves a total monarchy because of it.

Sperling nodded at last. "You know what to do with him." He didn't move from his position.

The escort dismounted, and Yerington told Jeb to do the same. Other men had piled out of the bunkhouse and come over. Jeb gave them a flat, indifferent stare, betraying nothing of his increasing concern. They marched him across the big yard to an open-ended shed and stopped there. Some of the men looked up at the brace running wall to wall overhead. The conviction knifed through him that they would hang him as Cash had warned and he had feared.

They hit him in a rushing pack, carrying him to the ground in a breath-gusting crash. He belted out and used his legs and feet and half a dozen men were needed to spread-eagle him, face down on the scuffed earth. He

12

was thus held helpless while a man made looped buck-skin strips into knots that cut into the roots of his thumbs. Then they jerked him upright again. A puncher tossed a rope over the beam above them while another fastened the other end to the thumb grips. Three of them began to pull.

Hock Sperling had come forward to watch the procedure with those grey glacial eyes. Jeb's arms swung over his head, then he was lifted until the toes of his boots barely reached the ground. His weight had to be divided between that and the tearing grip on his swelling thumbs. The other end of the rope was tied to a brace on the wall.

"I took you—by myself, Sperling," Jeb managed to gasp. "You need lots of help—at your age, I guess—"

Sperling spun on his heel and went back to the office.

Something about the taunt began to work on the punchers. Yerington walked off and the others soon drifted away. Jeb tried to divide his weight between the balls of his feet and the joints of his thumbs. Yet pain already licked along his arms from stretched ligaments and tormented flesh. When he tried to ease this with his feet, cramps soon assaulted his calves.

His jaw clenched until his teeth seemed about to crumble. He felt sweat crack through the dust on his face. His breath began to rip in and out in hurting sobs. He knew they might let him hang like this for a long while, and a fear began to work through the torture. Cash would know he had been brought here. He was sure to round up the other nesters and try to help. That would bring on a bloodier fight than had begun at Battle Creek. Maybe Sperling hoped it would happen, permitting a raging showdown in which the nesters could be called the aggressors.

He was helpless to prevent it. All he could do was hang, either resting his weight on his red-hot thumbs or the aching tips of his feet. The pain flowed into his shoulders, down his sides and sickened his viscera. His head grew so heavy he could no longer keep it from rocking limply forward.

It seemed ages that he remained so, helpless and raging, before he heard the sound he dreaded. Then it came to him that only one horse made that beat on the lead-in road from Sperling Creek. The horse came around the corner of a building presently. Through pain-bleared eyes he saw it was ridden by a slip of a girl.

She noticed him at the same time and shock leaped into her face. She quirted the horse and brought it whirling up to him. She cried out in an angry, carrying voice.

"What's going on here? Grandpa! Lot!"

Sperling hurried out of the office. His riders reappeared in the yard, all seeming taken back by her arrival. She threw herself from the saddle and ran up to the old man.

"Who's he?" she said furiously. "And what are you doing to him?"

"Now, Penny," Sperling said doggedly. "He asked for it and never you mind. Just get on in the house where you belong."

"I will not. Tell them to let him down, Grandpa."

"I said for you to stay out of this."

Lot Yerington shifted his feet uneasily. "He's right, Miss Penny. This Pelton used him something shameful this morning. We aim to teach him better."

"Pelton?"

"Claims to be the brother of that dead nester."

She swung to stare at Jeb then whirled toward the watching punchers. "I'm going to let him down. Anybody feel like stopping me?"

They stirred restlessly when she went over to where the rope was tied to the brace. Sperling, glowering but uncertain, shook his head at them. She pulled the loop out of the knot, and Jeb came down in a heap. Pain roiled through him again, and he found himself unable to rise. He heard the girl's voice again.

"Untie and help him up. Move, I say."

They freed him, but he shoved them away when they tried to lift him to his feet. After a moment he got to a weaving stand under his own power. "Thanks, ma'am," he managed to say. "More for the nesters' sake than mine. I think they wanted to bait them into an attack as an excuse to wipe them out."

"I wouldn't be surprised." Penny looked at Sperling haughtily, raking him with her eyes. "I spend one night

14

in town, and you let your men run wild. I apologize for him, Jeb Pelton. I suppose your horse is around somewhere."

"Yes, ma'am."

"Can you ride?"

"I can."

"Get his horse, Lot," she said. "Immediately."

She had them buffaloed, but only because they were caught in an act too ugly for a woman's eyes, with no taste for persisting now that she was on hand to object so strongly. When his head cleared Jeb took a better look at her, seeing how pretty she was. Although she wore a wool cap and short coat against the cold grey day, he could see that her hair was yellow and her body trim and slender, and he judged her to be about twenty years old. She seemed to have the headlong will of Sperling himself, but in her case grace tempered it.

A puncher came up with the P-D horse and handed the reins to Jeb, hostile still, but cautious. Yerington muttered a final warning. "You got off this time but there'll be another."

Jeb swung across the horse and rode out.

He was nearly at the junction of the north road when three horsemen spilled out of the gap between the mountains on ahead. He reined in while he made sure one of them was Cash. Then he waved his hat over his head to identify himself and rode toward them. It was as he had expected. Cash had gone driving through the gap to Head Creek to get help from Trace Getty, whose spread was on the far side. They had picked up Jimmy Hooker, another mesa nester, and the three had headed back for Dollarmark on the double.

From the rage painting their faces, Jeb knew he had to play down what had happened to him or they would still barrel into the big outfit. "Might have had a rough time," he said mildly, "but a chit of a girl rode in and broke it up. She made them turn me loose."

"That'd be Penny Baker," Cash said, and some of the savagery left him.

"She's got plenty of gumption."

"Her share and more." Cash laughed, and the tension was broken. "There was a pot of coffee me and Jeb left

15

when the ball opened, boys. How about helping us finish it?"

"If there ain't going to be a fracas," Hooker said, "I better get back to my work." Like the other two, he was young, and a shaggy edge of straw-colored hair showed under his worn hat. His eyes were a washed-out blue, but they met a man's steadily.

"Reckon I'll take you up on it, myself," Getty said to Cash. "I wanted to see Jeb, anyhow."

Hooker turned back into the gap and the others rode on toward Battle Creek. In another hour they were seated at the table Jeb and Cash had left so precipitately. Cash kindled a new fire in the stove to heat the coffee pot.

Getty was a tall, quick-moving man who ran a loner outfit on Head Creek. Excitement still danced in his brown eyes, and it was apparent that he liked trouble. He said, "I'm sure glad to see you here, Jeb. Cash told me he'd wired you about Tom. No need to say how the rest of us feel about that. He never gave Sperling the slightest excuse for it."

"Sperling never needed one," Cash said. "The sheriff couldn't get to first base running down the bushwhacker, in spite of what we told him. So Dollarmark had nothing to worry about."

Getty shrugged. "Well, we're movin' into winter, and that'll upset their wagon."

"How come?" Jeb said.

"I guess you never visited this country except in summer. It's the way the land around here lays. The winds come down from Idaho and pile up on the Sapphires and Dogleg and the mercury falls out of the thermometer. On the mesa across the mountains we're spared that. Dogleg juts out and forms a kind of horseshoe with the Sapphires that protects us. That means Dollarmark's got to get the mesa back before that kind of weather blows in or Hock Sperling's up the crick without a paddle."

"Why?"

"Cash never told you about the herd Sperling bought this fall?"

Jeb shook his head. "I only hit Broken Rock yesterday noon. Been a trifle busy since."

The others laughed. Getty said, "Well, Sperling brought in a big Oregon herd about a month back and played into our hands. It's like this. We always stood on the grounds that he didn't have the steers to use as much range as he once claimed. So to offset that argument he bought more steers. Just got where he could afford it and borrowed money at that. The hitch for him is this. If he can't put part of them on the mesa to winter, he's got to carry every head he owns on this side. Crowded the way he is, them northers'll ruin him. Even if he got the plateau away from us, he'd have to get the mesa, too. And he can't get either one, can he, Cash?"

"I sure hope not," Cash said.

Getty's face darkened. "Sometimes you sound like Tom used to. You going to tuck your tail between your legs because of what happened to him?"

"Just a minute," Jeb said. "Tom was a good-natured fellow, but he never run from a fight."

"I never meant it that way," Getty said hastily. "But some of the boys took to gloomin' when that new herd showed up, him with 'em. They just never thought the thing through."

"If you have, I'd like to know why you're so confident."

"For good reason," Getty said, amiable again. "Sperling's dodged going to law about us because he knows he'd lose the case. We've held out against him up to now, and if we can keep it up one more winter, it will hurt him so bad he'll be forced into court or leave us be. If he laws, it'll be settled in our favor, and he won't have a leg left to stand on."

"What makes you think it'll be settled your way?"

"This country's changed since the day he run it," Getty said with assurance, "and it's people like us that changed it. There's big outfits left but we out-vote 'em, and we make up most of the jury list. Sperling knows that himself, which is why he stuck to the old way of doing—just tryin' to run us out."

Jeb nodded. For years the new railroads had filled

17

the West with settlers who by weight of numbers now dominated politics and the courts. Dollarmark's rights in Sperling Basin were undisputed because Sperling had bought up a lot of railroad land and paid taxes on it. But the open range he once controlled was another matter, and the new people were bound to see it that way.

"Looks like you've got it figured, Getty," he agreed. "But it seems silly for him to light a fire under himself. Which is what he did when he bought that extra herd without knowing if he could put it on range occupied by you nesters."

Getty shook his head. "No, he had to have the extra stuff before he could justify himself. It brings his book count up to the old mark and he can say he's entitled to all his old holdings, which he never did give up his right to. How about you, Jeb? Want to throw in with us?"

Jeb shook his head, in doubt rather than negation. "All I can say is I want the man who killed Tom. If it takes all winter to nail him, I'll be here all winter. And you ought to know whose side I'm on already."

The coffee was ready and Cash set up cups and filled them. When the others started to roll cigarettes, Jeb followed suit automatically and wished he hadn't. He spilled the tobacco out of the paper when he tried to roll it and couldn't conceal the mishap. Cash reached over and grasped his wrist, turning the hand around, staring at the swollen, discolored thumb. His face went black.

"I thought you were hiding them things!" he exploded. "So they pulled that old Apache stunt on you!"

Getty took a hard look at the tormented thumb. When he saw the anger boiling in their faces, Jeb said, "Cut it out. I played a game with Dollarmark and you two weren't in on it."

"One more thing for 'em to pay for, though," Getty said bitterly.

Jeb leaned forward. "Listen, Getty, you said you hope to force Sperling into court. When you do it you better come in with your own hands clean. The more ill will he stirs up the better for you."

"We never lasted this long," Getty said grumpily, "letting them get away with things." He downed the rest of

18

his coffee and rose to his feet. "Well, I better ride. Drop over to Head Creek sometime, Jeb."

"I'll do that."

When the mesa nester had ridden out, Jeb said, "Tom didn't like him, eh? Getty seemed kind of hostile about him."

"Trace got on Tom's nerves, I guess," Cash said, shaking his head. "I admit he's got a pretty high opinion of himself, but so far he's delivered the goods. I ain't cared to coax you, Jeb. But if you should take up Tom's interest in this sorry spread we had, I'd feel better about its chance to stay in business."

When he saw the hope in the nester's eyes, Jeb's mind closed like a steel trap. He shared Tom's feeling about Trace Getty. The man made him uneasy although he couldn't put a finger on the reason, and the nesters were depending on his leadership entirely, throwing their lives as well as their possessions into the gamble.

"I'll be around long enough," he promised, "that I think I'll ride back to Broken Rock. I only took a short leave of absence from the company. I want to wire them to make it indefinite."

Cash grinned. "That's good to hear. You want company?"

"You've got work, and I know my way around well enough."

"When'll you be back?"

"Likely not till tomorrow."

Jeb borrowed a fresh horse from Cash, saddled it and rode out on the prairie trail to Broken Rock, following a road the nesters had established to avoid passing Dollarmark on the main route along Sperling Creek. The day was drawing to its close, the greyness deepening and the chill increasing. Was he about to give up a job that paid two-fifty a month for a meager, uncertain living wrung from a two-bit cattle spread?

He and his brother had been little alike in temperament. Tom had been drawn to the cattle outfits scattered in lonely places, while Jeb took naturally to the lively, dangerous life of the mining camps and express trails. But a time came when too much of that palled on a man, he had discovered. Maybe he needed to build something

19

outside himself and a bank account, something that—as
Tom had done—he would slave and starve and die for if
necessary.

Chapter 3

THE LAMPLIGHTER was passing down the long street of
Broken Rock, lifting his taper to the dusty globes, when
Jeb rode down the bridge. Forward a black, cracked
rock bluff crowded the town against the railroad tracks
and sluggish, twisting river. The last late beef waited in
the stockpens above town to load out for Omaha. Freight
outfits from ranches and mining camps in the enormous
hinterland stood ranked in the wagon yard. A railroad
hand on a one-man speeder pulled his patient way in
from the west to derail for the night by the freight shed.

Jeb stopped at the depot and filed his wire, reflecting
that in a space of twelve unpredictable hours he had
probably changed the course of his life. He paid for the
telegram and walked out to the cinder platform, observing that a mercantile beyond the busy street was still
open for business. He went over. The establishment held
a thin crowd of nesters from the hay ranches along the
river and out in its concoursing valleys. They were family
men with weathered, patient wives and wild children.
They were the builders of a new age come to a river
that for two decades had run more cattle than any other
region between the Rockies and the Sierra.

A man waiting by the stove while his wife did her
buying gave him a nod. "Gettin' a mite cold out, ain't it?"

"Nights in this country're all too cold for a man from
the coast," Jeb said.

"You from Californy?"

"Randsburg. It's a Mojave town."

"I heard tell. Pretty tough place, I guess."

"I've seen worse. You raising hay?"

"Aim to when I get my ditches dug." The man's wife
looked around and motioned to him. "Well, here's where

20

I come in. She runs up the bill but I got to foot it." He walked over to her.

Jeb waited a while longer for his turn then bought tobacco and ammunition, adding some spare clothing he had not brought with him on the train. Carrying the purchases to his horse, he loaded his saddlebags and rode down to the livery barn. Afterward he registered at the hotel, having spent too many hours in the saddle that day to consider the long ride back to Battle Creek.

He had a steak and hashbrowns in a nearby eating house and was coming out the door when he saw a party of Dollarmark punchers ride past. They were noisy and in high spirits, bent only on a night in town. None of them noticed him. He frowned, not wanting to dodge them but not caring to let them resume their interrupted reprisal. He watched until they pulled in at the hitching rail in front of the saloon before he moved down the sidewalk.

He went into a sidestreet establishment, had a drink and bought a cigar. A group of oldsters were forming a card game and he walked over to them. He said, "Room for one more?"

A man glanced up. "Pretty tame game, but if you don't mind that draw up a chair."

He sat down in what developed into a poker session given mostly to good-natured banter. From their clothes, three were townsters killing a long cold evening. Another had the blistering vocabulary of a muleskinner from the freight trails. The one who caught Jeb's interest had the look and talk of a cowhand from way back.

"Ain't seen you around," this one said, once the game got going.

"Got off the eastbound yesterday. The name's Pelton."

"I'm Buck Gillidge. Till lately there was a Tom Pelton around here. I got to know him pretty well."

"He was my brother."

Gillidge gave him a close look. "Too bad about him. He was an all right hombre."

"Where'd you know him?"

"Till last spring I rode for Dollarmark."

Jeb's eyes narrowed. "And quit?"

21

"I'll say I did. Couldn't stomach the scum Hock Sperling took to putting on his payroll, so I drawed my time."

"You mean," the teamster said, "you didn't have the fighting sand Hock wants, so he tied a can to your tail."

Gillidge gave him a look of sour indifference and the game resumed. They were cronies, whiling away the night, and nobody was ever much ahead or behind. Jeb sat in for a couple of hours, finding their company pleasant, then he excused himself. Gillidge threw in his hand at the same time.

"Buy you a drink?" Jeb said.

"Don't mind if you do."

They went over to the uncrowded bar. The old man was silent for a moment, bleakly thoughtful. Finally he said, "Looks like you sprained your thumbs."

"Maybe I tried to crack a coconut."

"I seen Hock Sperling pull that stunt on more'n one rustler in my time. Usually it discouraged 'em."

"Tends to have that effect, but I wasn't rustling. He got Injun blood?"

"A man'd think so. Still, Hock ain't so bad. He's only mean when he's crossed, and he's got his soft side."

"One's that granddaughter, I suppose."

"You know Penny?"

"Hardly, but she saved me a rough time, and I take my hat off to her. Which doesn't soften my opinion of Sperling a bit."

"Well, he's got his reasons," Gillidge said doggedly. "The way he sees it, he dassn't let them nesters stay. The country's fillin' with 'em, and they'd have the whole shebang in a few years more. So he's hired him a crew that'll help stall that off. I never blamed him, even if I didn't want a part in it myself."

"You're forgetting that the nesters have a side, too."

"No, I ain't. I feel downright sorry for 'em, particularly Cash Donovan. He likely never told you but he's gone on Penny, and she likes him pretty well, too. Yet he's got to fight her granddad to hold what he considers his'n, which makes a hot seat."

Jeb swung toward him, his eyes hard. "That's something Sperling would like even less than Cash's squat-

22

ting. Maybe Tom just got in the way of a bullet intended for Cash."

"Well, it's possible. It wouldn't be Hock's doin', but he sure wouldn't mourn if somethin' took Cash out of the picture. Hock's got one or two hard cases who'd do it if they got a chance, just to try and curry favor with the old boy."

"Name me a couple, Buck."

"No, I won't point the finger at any man. It was your guess, not mine, and damned wild at that." Gillidge swung away then turned back. "Thanks for the likker. Anything I can do for you, let me know. I'm ridin' a chair here in town this winter." He went out.

Jeb paid for the drinks and moved to the door. Night had come down three hours ago but he stepped into a still active street. Yardhands from the stock pens, railroad employees and townspeople stood about or passed along the twin walks that ran parallel to the river. The stores had closed but the saloons were doing a boom business. Most of the tie-rails were still festooned with saddlehorses.

He hadn't reached the first crosswalk when he heard a man in a group he had passed speak in a rising voice, "Say, ain't that Jeb Pelton?"

He disdained to look back, but nervous energy kicked through him while he walked on to the corner. The agitation increased behind him. A man called, "Hey, Trig, here's Pelton!" and he knew that in a minute Dollarmark would be on his heels in force. He turned the corner, still walking calmly, passed down to the end of the building there and stepped into the darker space in its rear. Shouts bucked along the street, drawing closer. They had seen him turn off the main thoroughfare.

He stood with his hand on his gun, sharp with desire to challenge them. It couldn't be done without spreading gunplay, which he was too old a hand at to want in a busy town. They would check the hotel presently, see his name on the register, so the best thing was to avoid them until he could leave town unseen.

Two men came along the walk from the main street, their heels hammering the planks. There was too much chance of their checking this alley, and Jeb slid deeper

23

into the darkness. A back yard appeared on his left, with two or three sheds then a house that fronted the parallel street. He vaulted the fence and entered the yard. His hunch paid off, for he heard them turn into the alley where he had been. He dashed to the nearest and biggest shed. Its door was closed but not locked. He stepped in.

He was aware of increased warmth and when he looked about he saw a red glow in the deep end of the place. This wasn't a blacksmith shop but the trapped smells made it appear to be a forge back there. Dollarmark was searching the alley as they went through. He shut the door.

The Sperling punchers passed on to the far end of the alley and did some shouting to somebody from there. It wouldn't do to make for the livery barn and his horse just yet. He moved farther into the shed, curious about that fire, and collided violently with something unseen. It went over, setting up a racket he thought would carry across the town. He froze in his tracks, cursing himself for not staying put.

Whoever came across the yard did it so silently he wasn't aware of anything until the door burst open. Lantern light fell into the gloomy interior, and he saw the barrel of a rifle then, to his surprise, a skirted figure. She saw him at the same time and the gun came up to her side, lined on him squarely.

"What are you doing in here?" she said angrily.

She was young, dark, and according to the lantern light, very pretty. She wore a cotton housedress, slim at the waist and flaring to her feet, and since she had no wrap she must have come out of the dwelling next door. She took a step closer, the gun still threatening him.

"Answer me."

He recovered his wits to say, "I'm not prowling, ma'am. Those men out there are looking for me, and I don't want to see 'em."

"What do they want you for?"

"Well, they're Dollarmark hands, and they don't happen to like me."

She closed the door quickly, which was some reassurance. But she kept the gun on him as she came farther toward him. He looked about, puzzled. He had knocked over a bench in the darkness and spilled a lot of vases and pitchers that now lay on the floor in various degrees of ruin. The glow had come from something that looked like an assayer's muffle furnace except that it was larger.

"What're you running here?" he said.

"That's a kiln. I make pottery, and it appears you spoiled some very nice pieces I threw today. They were drying so I could bisque them."

"Golly, I—"

"You haven't told me what Dollarmark's got against you," she said.

"I'm Jeb Pelton, ma'am. My brother was an old hand around here, but I just got in yesterday. And found myself in an argument with Hock Sperling's outfit right off. Some of them recognized me a while ago and took after me again. I don't care to start throwing lead here in town."

"Are you Tom Pelton's brother?"

He nodded. "Did you know him?"

She lowered the rifle at last. Her expression softened. "And I know about the trouble. I'm sorry I was so nasty, but some of the town bums know this place is often warm at night so they sneak in here to sleep. I have a brother on Muleshoe Mesa. I'm Anita Toinbee."

He looked puzzled for there was no wedding band on her hand. "Don't remember hearing that name."

"You wouldn't. He's Trace Getty, my half-brother actually."

"Oh, sure. I saw him today."

There was more shouting and again it was right at hand. Dollarmark's earnest search seemed to have drawn some town sports into its wake, for the commotion was livelier. He saw a quick worry in Anita's eyes.

Looking back at him, she said, "There's nothing unusual about a light in this shed at night. When I fire I have to keep it going till it's done. That's why I'm cold-hearted about bums. I dislike stumbling onto them in the scary hours of the morning."

"Don't want to get you into trouble, and they might start searching buildings."

25

She pointed. "If they come around here, that clay bin will hold you, and I'll take care of the rest."

Except for sharing Getty's dark complexion there was no resemblance between him and this remarkable girl. She struck him as much finer texture, and her artistic bent was surely something the rough mesa nester did not share. She had a cool, tough courage herself, but it was acceptant rather than aggressive. He wondered if there were other members of the family in the house and what she did with all the pottery and how well she had known Tom. Yet this was hardly the place for idle talk and he said nothing. He didn't want to leave the place in such a mess and went over to pick up the pieces of her ruined handwork.

She said, "Never mind. They probably weren't as good as I hoped, anyway. One day I throw something I think it's the best ever. The next day it looks like another abused wad of clay."

He laughed. "You sure have a fancy for those things." He looked at a shelf of finished pottery that had already been glazed in the kiln. "Where can you use all of 'em?"

"Oh, I sell them in San Francisco. And get a rather fancy price, too."

"They sure please the eye."

"Thank you."

He went ahead and cleaned up the mess anyway, dumping the debris in a trash can. The sounds of pursuit had faded once more. "I'm glad you panned out on my side."

"Is it safe for you to leave so soon?"

"I'll pick up my horse at the livery and hit for the nester country."

"Good luck."

"Same to you, ma'am, and thanks."

He stepped out into the yard and paused to keen the night. Passing back into the alley, he turned right, walking quietly. Since they hadn't found his horse on the street they would have checked the livery, and there would be somebody laying in wait for him there. He crossed a side street and slipped into another alley. He could see the back of the livery barn on ahead, faint stripes of light showing through the cracks in the wall.

The structure backed onto a gully that accommodated its manure pile. He crossed the depression and came up to the barn's back opening.

The door stood ajar and he stepped in, catching the heavy smells of animals, harness and old hay. A lantern swung at the center of the wide street door on ahead and from his position it outlined two men waiting alertly deeper in. A hack had been rolled into a space on his right, probably a rental rig, and he slipped over to it. Feeling in the bed, he found a hub wrench which he tossed out into the darkness. It struck something solid and made a thump when it fell.

The men up there whirled and came toward him, instantly hostile. He waited in the darkness, his breath checked. When they came abreast he stepped out into the pale light. He had fisted his gun.

"Hold up, gents, and swallow your tongues."

They hauled around, saw him and settled in their tracks. He had seen them at Dollarmark, and one's mouth and throat made the spasmodic motion of a suppressed yell. They remembered him, too.

"Where's the hostler?" Jeb said.

"In his office."

"Head for it. Fast."

They led him into the barn office where a stablehand sat nodding by the stove. He wasn't belligerent toward Jeb but prudence had counseled him to a course of neutrality in the argument with Dollarmark. He came awake with a start, straightening in the chair.

"It's all right," Jeb said. "Saddle my horse and fetch him up here."

"Sure."

The man ducked out. Jeb put a flat stare on the Sperling riders. Old Buck Gillidge had mentioned quitting the big outfit because of the low calibre men it was hiring. This pair was representative. They watched him sullenly, shifting their feet. They still wanted to raise an outcry, but his gun blocked the impulse.

A few minutes passed before the hostler came back in. "Ready to ride," he said.

"Thanks." Jeb drew a couple of dollars from his pocket and handed them over. He cut a glance to the others.

"I'll watch this place till I'm around the corner. If you show yourself you're on your way to Boot Hill." He backed out.

He swung into the saddle, walked the horse to the exit, and a moment later was safely around the corner onto a side street. Instead of heading directly for Battle Creek as they would expect, he made his way to the river road for a roundabout but prudent ride home.

Chapter 4

A COLD SNAP had come on in the night following Jeb's return to Battle Creek after the brush with Dollarmark in Broken Rock. The dawn had held a freezing fog the Indians called *pogonip*. The desert brush still glittered with its crystals, patches of weighty vapor lay in the hallows and a dull cheerlessness spread over the wild land of the Humboldt Valley.

Jeb stopped at the point where Cash had found Tom after his horse reached home with an empty saddle. He studied the upthrust of black rock where the bullet must have come from and speculated on the killer's probable route of escape when the deed was accomplished. He was well down Battle Creek from headquarters. Below him was the line fence Sperling had run to hold nester stock off a strip of railroad land he owned along the river.

Dollarmark's hostility and this proximity to its holdings were the sum of the evidence against the big outfit. All other sign had been obliterated by the heavy rain falling at the time of the killing. Yet the anger that had carried him deep into the situation already would not let him give up. He had to discover the precise identity of his brother's murderer, even if Tom had been mistaken for Cash Donovan.

He rode onto the scab and took another exhaustive look about. He hoped against hope for that bit of luck that sometimes caused something to be dropped or imprinted at the scene of a crime, something that would give him even the scantiest clue. He saw the paper from several cigarettes that had been smoked and discarded, beaten flat and the tobacco washed aside. A million men in the West used that particular brown paper. It meant only that the killer was a heavy smoker. He would also be acquainted with Tom's daily rounds and according to Cash one or the other had ridden the creek to the line fence every day. Dollarmark's own routine would familiarize them all with that fact without pointing to any individual Sperling rider.

As to the escape afterward, the killer could have cut across the hump immediately and faded out on Dollarmark range in Sperling Basin. Or he could have struck the creek road to town. Tom's horse had come in riderless around four in the afternoon, and Cash estimated that the shooting happened an hour earlier. That furnished a hypothesis although it offered little hope.

The man could have left the big ranch in the guise of going to town, detoured long enough to make the waylay, then gone on. If it could be determined that such a Dollarmark man had been in Broken Rock in late afternoon that day, Jeb reflected, he might have established an important earmark or so. The saloon keepers would be apt to know, the postmaster, or old Buck Gillidge might have noticed since he was an old Sperling hand himself. It had been stormy that day. The murder and the storm on the same day might help people to remember.

He was about a third of the way to town already, so he rode on in. The saloons and post office produced nothing, and he couldn't locate Gillidge. He thought of one other who might have recognized someone from Sperling Basin—if she circulated much in the town. Besides, if he wasn't flattering himself, Anita Toinbee might like to know, anyway, that he had got out of town all right that night. He rode to her house.

No one responded to his knock on the door but for luck he went around back, where he found her in the workshop. She wore jeans and an old shirt now and was splattered with wet clay smudges and flung dirty water.

29

"Oh—I look like a tramp," she said, coloring, "but I can't help it when I'm throwing new stuff."

"What're you doing there?" he said, looking at the potter's wheel on which she sat.

"Trying to raise a piece to sixteen inches and break my own record. I'm glad you made out all right the other night."

"I come with a question. Do you recall the day Tom was killed?"

She looked startled. "Sure. It was a week ago yesterday, the day I sent a tea set to San Francisco. Also the day Trace comes in to have supper with me. Moreover, I remember, it was raining pitchforks."

"Tracy Getty?" Jeb said, surprised. "He came in that day?"

She nodded. "We're all that's left of the family, and I get pretty lonesome."

"Well, I was looking for somebody on the other side of the fence. A Sperling hand who might have been in town late that same day."

She mused a moment. "Let's see. I went to the store to pick up some things for supper. I remember that my umbrella blew inside out. But I don't remember seeing so much as a Dollarmark horse on the street. I'd notice because I grew up in this country."

"Guess I was chasin' a fast rabbit, anyhow," Jeb admitted. "Making an excuse to see you, maybe."

"Well, thanks. How's it going out there?"

"Quiet at the moment." He liked her brown eyes, the first time he had seen them in daylight, and the wild curl of her thick dark hair. Her face was extremely sensitive, and little thoughts and feelings flickered there to pique a man's own mind. The mud-streaked jeans showed him a neat slenderness of waist and thigh. The pleasant thought kicked through him that she was the kind of girl he'd been on the lookout for.

"You're looking for the man who killed Tom," she said. "I suppose you'll kill him if you find him."

"I reckon."

She shrugged. "I guess there's no talking a man out of a drive like that." The thought displeased her, and she added quickly, "Like to see what I'm doing? This

30

would be a gorgeous vase or pitcher if I could raise it high enough."

"That thing?" All he saw was a nearly shapeless lump of wet clay on the wheel head.

"Wait. I've spoiled two this morning and was just starting over." She began to kick the heavy wooden flywheel at the bottom of the shaft, spinning the head and its tawny burden. She dipped her hands in a pan of muddy water and seemed to forget him completely.

Her skill astonished him. The glistening, whirling clay quit wobbling as she centered it on the head with cupped, expert hands. Her thumbs and fingers did something and the lump began to hollow out. Thick walls started to rise under her steady, coaxing hands. Her head cocked to the side and the tip of her tongue crept between her lips. She had that look of intense concentration usually encountered only in children. It delighted him.

Sometimes she stopped to dip her fingers and give the wheel a few more kicks. The walls rose higher, grew thinner, and she smoothed the spinning outer surface with a rib. The thing was first a big tube that broadened and developed a belly, then began to come in again to form a neck.

She glanced up and her speckled face was hopeful, then she was lost in the work again. She raised on the footrests for the last steps to get more reach. Nearly shaped, the piece had climbed to what he thought was almost her goal of sixteen inches. Then the clay lurched, wobbled crazily and collapsed soggily on the spinning head.

"Damn," she said furiously. "It does that even when I'm not trying to show off."

"Nearly had it, though."

"I've nearly had it fifty times, Jeb Pelton."

He left her to consider the error of her ways and walked out to his waiting horse. He rode across the bridge and headed for Battle Creek, weighted by defeat, yet naggingly crowded toward the man he had to find. Since he knew that he might be watched and followed now, he again took the river road. The detour would let him see the rest of the disputed Dogleg plateau,

31

a section he had not frequented on his few visits to see Tom.

The river ran beside him, lazy and twisting. Once its guidance of travelers had been the only feature of all Nevada considered of any value. Trappers had been the first white men to follow it, and Mormons had travelled beside it, setting up their outpost in Carson Valley, and a hundred thousand goldseekers had scurried along its alkali margins on their way to California. The transcontinental had laid steel rails beside the wagon tracks, and longhorns came from Texas, and the great desert valley had become a thing to be fought over bitterly.

He reached the mouth of Battle Creek and followed the stream across country until he cut the prairie road that swung on toward Sagehen and Squaw Creeks. The country he entered was a repetition of the plateau farther south and rose in the same lapping swells to splash against the bulwark of Dogleg Mountains. The transecting creek valleys were separated only by thin breaks that were no barrier to free travel and grazing. When he topped over and looked down at the tame little Sagehen in the lower ground he saw the ranch structures of Swede Jorgan. The setup was somewhat larger than Cash and Tom had been able to afford on Battle Creek. He rode down to the place.

Two men were dressing out a beef hung at the open end of a shed. They turned hastily for he had come in on the blind side of the trees. He grinned at them, saying, "Howdy. I'm Jeb Pelton, in case you don't remember."

Their expressions softened. One was a powerful, square-headed man of middle age, and this was Jorgan, whom Jeb had met. He said, "Sure I remember you, Jeb. Light down and rest your saddle. This here's Leet Teebo from Squaw Creek. We were getting a little fresh meat."

"Not slow elk off Sperling, I hope." Jeb swung down and shook hands.

"Sperling's accused us of it, sure enough," Teebo said. He was tall and skinny but had the look of cool assurance that Jorgan possessed. They covered the beef

32

with a tarp to protect it. Jorgan nodded toward the house.

"Weather's so nippy, me and Leet could stand warmin' up too, Jeb. Let's go in."

They repaired to the house where a fire burned in an old cast-iron stove. There was coffee already cooked, and Jorgan poured it into cups. "I aimed to get down to see you, Jeb," he said. "Sure a shame about Tom. Getty told me they shot up you and Cash the other day to boot."

"There was a little bickering, all right."

"Getting to be a pretty big bickering," Teebo said dryly. "Trace says you ain't decided whether to stick around with us."

"Guess I'll be here a while, all right."

"Good. What I hear, we need you, now that we've lost Tom."

"Got any idea who killed him?"

"Dollarmark."

"That's not good enough. I want the son that actually threw the lead."

Jorgan lighted the pipe he had stuffed. "Well, we could narrow it down some, I guess. Sperling didn't have any angels in his outfit before he started hiring gunslingers but most of the old hands were above an outright bushwhackin'."

"Who's the worst of the new lot?"

Jorgan glanced at Teebo, "Who'd you say, Leet?"

"Well, Trig Godfrey and Alf Heater could spot a skunk the first squirt and still outstink him."

Jeb fixed the names in mind. "How about Lot Yerington?"

"Cut off the same bolt as Hock," Jorgan said. "Been his ramrod for years. Sees things the old way and sure does 'em the old way, too. Yet I reckon if he aimed to kill a man he'd stand up and face him."

That was the impression Jeb had got from Cash, and he wondered how these two nesters felt about Getty. He said, "I hear Getty's sort of led you boys in fighting off Dollarmark. He strikes me as a pretty capable man."

Teebo grinned. "I reckon he's got what the rest of us lack, and that's brains."

Jorgan nodded. "That's right. When Sperling brought in them new steers, the rest of us thought we ought to force a showdown out of him. Trace showed us how to use our heads and them extra steers to beat Hock at his own game, or let bad weather do it."

"How long before that kind of weather comes?"

"Won't be more than a few weeks till it's cold enough to do some damage."

"Sperling's aware of that danger."

"Sure," Jorgan agreed, "but what can he do about it?"

"I imagine he took it into consideration before he committed himself to take care of so many extra steers."

"Nobody thinks we'll have a picnic," Teebo said, "but we're bettin' on Trace to match anything Sperling can think of."

They were solidly behind Getty, Jeb saw, and he wished the mesa nester didn't make him feel uneasy. He rode out presently and came in on Battle Creek to receive a surprise. A horse wearing the Dollarmark shoulder brand stood in front of the house. Jeb's brow knit as he rode forward, alert and puzzled; then he noticed the short stirrups and his worry eased. The door opened and Cash stood there with the rifle in his hands. Hock Sperling's granddaughter looked out uneasily behind him.

"Oh, it's you," Cash said in relief. "Come on in."

Jeb dismounted and moved into the house and shut the door. He hooked his hat on a wall peg and said, "How are you, Penny?" recalling what Gillidge had said about the interest these two had in each other. He hung his coat beside the hat, knowing he had interrupted a tryst.

"Very well, thank you," the girl said. Her cheeks were red.

Jeb grinned. "At ease, you two. You may be on different sides, but if you can be friends I'm for it."

Cash grinned and Penny's face broke into a smile. Without the coat and cap she had worn the other day he could tell how slender and splendidly formed she was.

"I reckon it's more'n friends," Cash said. "Anyhow, on my side."

34

"You show sense. If it wasn't for her I'd have thumbs a foot long now."

They laughed, and the tension was gone.

"I'm sorry about that," Penny said. "I learned afterward why they did it. I don't think my grandfather could be guilty of what you accused him of, Jeb, and you did humiliate him dreadfully."

"I never called him guilty. But he was sure responsible."

She glanced away, badgered and vulnerable. "I suppose so. He's got some dreadful men working for him. But I wish you'd consider this. He believes he's in the right in the range trouble. He follows his truth the same as you do."

"Maybe. But there's no excuse for his methods."

She lifted her head. "Well, if one of his men killed your brother, I'd never believe he ordered it. He's not that bad."

"But he's responsible, the same as for that insult to Tom's grave."

"Have it your way." She turned to Cash. "I've got to go now."

The tall puncher frowned but moved to where her coat lay over the back of a chair. He helped her into it, and Jeb stayed where he was when they went outdoors.

When Cash returned, he said tartly, "No need to jump down her throat about it."

"I didn't. But I'm tired of that line. Buck Gillidge gave me the same thing in town the other evening. It gravels me, that's all."

"Well, I go along with you there. But it's hard for Penny or Buck to see Sperling like we do. They're too close, and she's unhappy enough."

"She ready to marry you?"

Cash shrugged. "Maybe, but I won't ask her till this trouble's settled. My lease on life ain't strong enough."

"That reminds me. Buck told me about you two, and I wondered if Tom wasn't killed by mistake for you."

"Could be. It's another thing Sperling wouldn't order done, but he wouldn't grieve any if I got eliminated in the fracas."

35

Chapter 5

HOCK SPERLING threw another cedar log on the blaze and stood bent, staring at the rugged rock fireplace, listening to the wind split on the house corners and gauging the night that lay ahead. The last cattle had drifted down from the hills, and he was ready to move decisively against his enemies. It had been a long and bitter wait of nearly five years. He broke off his study and looked about, restless and disturbed but in no wise relenting in his purpose.

The long living room was rustic, hung with antlers, animal heads and guns, and the floors were covered with woven rugs, with a few deer and bear skins added. The furniture was massive, made by the carpenters who built the rambling log house. His glance slid up to the open gallery and paused on the closed door of Penny's room. A thought raked through his brain that made him wince. He was losing her. Maybe he had lost her already.

He went back to his chair and picked up the cigar he had laid down a moment before. A knock that he recognized sounded on the door, and he called, "Come in, Lot," and Yerington walked in, his shoulders hunched from the galling wind. The foreman went straight to the fire and stood with his back to it, looking down at the old man. Among the vast uncertainties of the world, one thing was sure, Sperling reflected. Lot Yerington would die for Dollarmark, just as he had lived for it down through the years.

"It's all set, Hock," Yerington said.

Sperling nodded. "All right. Mind you, there's to be no unnecessary rough stuff tonight. Place two men at each nester shack and tell 'em not to start anything themselves. But if a nester's alarmed or shows himself outside, they're to hold him till further orders. There'll

36

be two men at Donovan's, remember, with Pelton staying there."

Yerington tipped his head. "You coming along?"

"Naturally." Sperling looked at his watch. "It's half past ten. We'll start at eleven. Have my horse ready."

"Sure." Yerington went out.

Sperling glanced up at his granddaughter's door, wondering if she had eavesdropped. It didn't matter. She couldn't prevent it and would learn of it tomorrow anyway. He relighted the cigar, his eyes fixed on the fire again. Her hold on his affections had a triple strand, he mused. She was not only like her mother but also resembled her grandmother, Sperling's wife, making her remind him of two women he had loved and lost to the grim reaper. Yet she had got something foreign from her father, too, which gave her her own way of seeing things like this plague of nesters.

Listening again, Sperling cursed the wind, swept back by it to the two stock-killing winters that had so nearly destroyed the first Dollarmark. That had been a ranch! Two thousand longhorns he had trailed from Texas had been the start of it. He had fought Indians and outlaws, heat and drought, storms and stampedes on the road. He had turned the critters loose on Sperling Creek, that year, fought the same elements over again time after time, and as the years went by had become one of Nevada's first cattle barons. There were few left in the country who understood what all that had cost, why it gave him pride and satisfaction, why he would fight on to the end.

There had been encroachments before these nesters, by sheepmen and hostile cattle outfits. He couldn't count the times he had laid his life on the line as the price of possession. He had grown tough, and he had developed tough methods. He had paid the price in other ways, too, losing first his wife and then his daughter, both in childbirth. He had seen a fine son-in-law, Penny's father, trampled to death in a stampede, leaving him alone except for the angry girl shut in her room up there.

He glanced at his watch and saw that he had five minutes to get ready and join the men. Rising, he tossed the stub of his cigar into the fire, took a shell belt off the back of a chair and buckled it on. He wound a muffler around his neck, got into his heavy sheepskin and pulled on his hat. He took another brief look at Penny's door, then went out into the forbidding night.

The men waited with their horses, two dozen strong. Sperling said nothing as he walked to his own mount and swung into the saddle. Still silent, he led them out.

They followed the creek road to the north-leading branch just short of the gap to Muleshoe Mesa. Yerington dropped off a man, in case by mischance a warning reached the mesa, and its nesters tried to interfere. They stopped again a mile short of Battle Creek where the foreman tolled off three pairs.

"You know what to do," he informed them. "Keep 'em pinned down till you know it's over, and no rough stuff that ain't called for."

The men drifted forward, bound for the three nester shacks on as many plateau creeks. Sperling led the rest into the foothills of Dogleg Mountain. The nester cattle would all have drifted in by now, which was what he had waited for. He left men to sweep down the creek valley and continued to Sagehen where he dropped off Yerington with more. He took the rest on to Squaw Creek himself.

This was range Leet Teebo had usurped, taking advantage of Dollarmark's temporary weakness. Sperling scattered his men and told them to drive everything ahead of them until they came to the line fence far down the plateau. The wind knifed him painfully, but it would help cover any lowing by the moving cattle, and he could surely stand it if his riders could, even though they were much younger men.

The wind helped, also, in that the steers would be gathered in the lee of the breaks, under bluffs and in woody areas, making them easier to find. He followed the creek, skirting Teebo's house. It showed no light, but he knew his men were there by now, making sure there was no interference. He flushed a few steers out of the cutbanks along the Squaw, occasionally cutting to the side to throw a bunch from behind a flattop or out of a gully. Now and then he glimpsed a man off through the cold starlight, working half-blind but helping to clean Dollarmark's fouled range.

It took four hours of such zigzag riding for all of them to reach the line fence where the cattle were held up. He estimated the gather from this valley at around four hundred head, about what Teebo had tallied. He passed the word for the stuff to be drifted south along the line of the barbed wire. Past the 'tween-creek breaks they picked up Yerington, his crew and another and large cut of steers. These were Jorgan's cattle. The Battle Creek animals were snowballed into the growing herd, which was taken on past the end of the hump to the main creek road. There point riders turned them east toward the mountains. All had gone placidly, and Sperling hoped there had been no violence at the nester shacks. He had no compassion for his enemies but wanted as much justice on his side in this maneuver as he could manage.

The herd of now around fourteen hundred head strung out a long ways as it traveled along Sperling Creek toward the gap to Muleshoe Mesa. Sperling rode forward with Yerington and joined the man left previously at the yawning passage. They formed a fan and sat waiting, ready to thread the lead steers into the wide canyon. The wind's force compounded as it came down along the mountains from the north, cutting through clothes and tissue to the bone. The grumbling herd was far from sight yet and would take another hour to get there, Sperling estimated.

He sat with his memories, recalling more terrible nights five years ago when he and his men had fought to save the cattle. It had been a losing proposition but they had never given up, bucking the deep snows on half-dead horses, tailing up steers dropped by weakness, staggering to headquarters at long intervals to fall nearly dead from the saddle. Even when it wasn't snowing, the *pogonip* would be so thick a man could lose himself ten minutes away from headquarters. Three of his men had died in it all, another had lost a foot to frostbite. It seemed to him that he and they had won an indisputable right to this range.

Thus he mused while the long wait passed, then Yerington called sharply, "They're comin', Hock." He straightened in the saddle, again concentrating on the night's job. The point riders had aimed the herd accurately at the gap so that the fanners had little to do but hold their places. The first steers were swallowed in the passage, the others trailed meekly along, the lowing decreasing as the walls of the mountain passage cut them off from the wind. When the last had gone in, Sperling rode over to Yerington.

"I reckon that does it, Hock," Yerington said.

"As far as it goes."

"Yeah, I know."

Sperling felt no special satisfaction, only a sense of having done the necessary. The gap was about a mile long and they let the men take the herd on through and give it a running shove down Muleshoe Mesa. No combination of nesters could ever throw it back across to the plateau, Sperling mused. When the punchers had returned, he said, "I want two men guardin' this gap day and night. Better knock together some kind of shelter for 'em tomorrow, Lot. Now we've got our own stuff to move in."

It had been ready for days, the two thousand head of cattle he meant to put on the Dogleg plateau where the nester stuff had been. The nigh side of the mountains would still be dangerously crowded, but there was another move like this to come when the excess was finally moved to the mesa. The steers had been held on the south fork of Sperling Creek, and it was a simple business to chouse them north, dropping off a third at each of the creek valleys. The last of it was accomplished just as dawn cracked open the bitter night.

Sperling left the men with the cattle and rode alone up Squaw Creek to Swede Jorgan's house. Fatigue and cold reminded him sternly of his years. Yet he sat his saddle erectly, his body starched by the pride that had been high among the passions that had ruled his life. He drew near Jorgan's to see smoke whip down the wind from the chimney. That warned him that Jorgan had got onto the cattle movement. This was confirmed when one of his own men came to the shack door when he rode in. The puncher looked out worriedly but eased

40

when he saw Sperling. He came out into the yard.

"Get the stuff in place?" he said.

Sperling nodded. "What kind of trouble here?"

"None at all. The Swede slept like a baby all night. But when he come out for firewood this morning we figured we better take him."

Sperling nodded and rode up to the door, calling, "Jorgan!"

In a moment Swede Jorgan's big body was framed in the doorway. His eyes were murderous but he was mystified and uncertain.

"It's all over for you, Jorgan." Sperling snapped out the words. "My cattle are on the plateau to stay. You've got today to move your possessions out of here. If they're gone by night I'll buy your buildings. If they're not, I'll burn everything. The same goes for Teebo and Donovan. Tell 'em that."

Jorgan's voice was heavy. "What did you do with my steers?"

"They weren't hurt though they should have been. They've eaten my grass for years."

"Your grass! You God or somethin'? You own the whole of creation?"

"No use arguin' that point. I warned you people time and again you were trespassing on me, and your mangy cattle never were anything but strays."

"You won't get away with it!"

Sperling made a dismissing motion with his hand. "Just have your possessions gone by night if you don't want to lose 'em." He looked at his men. "Turn him loose. And you boys go down the crick and join the others."

He rode out without another word, striking across country toward the low, shrouded outline of the big hump. He crossed the high land about an hour later and dropped down to Sperling Basin. He rode the last couple of miles in deep weariness and came in on Dollarmark's headquarters.

Penny was up when he walked into the house. Her hair was in braids, she wore a robe, and he knew she had been there a good part of the night. She was sipping coffee and her tired eyes looked across the rim of the

41

cup at him, level and clean and focused in sharp accusation.

"Well, what happened last night?" she said when he did no more than grunt an acknowledgment of her presence. She put down the cup and watched him.

He hung up his coat and walked over to the fire, yearning to draw its heat into his chilled old body. "We moved the nester cattle off the plateau and put our'n on," he said finally.

"How many men were killed?"

"There was no gunplay."

"And you think there won't be? You suppose you're dealing with spineless fools?"

"I'm supposing nothing. I'm only standing on my rights and protecting my property."

"How can you be so certain it's yours?"

"I know it's mine!" he said explosively. "When I'm dead and it's yours, I don't give a hang what you do. While it's my concern I'll defend it to the last ditch."

"And the last life."

His anger ran in him violently, and he stood silent while he put it down. She sat for a while longer under his stony, withdrawn regard, then rose and went up the stairs to her room.

Sperling poured himself a stiff drink and returned to the fire. He felt too cold ever to be thoroughly warm again. Presently he pulled on his coat and walked across to the cookshack and ate some breakfast. Afterward he went to his office where a roust-about had kindled a fire in the potbelly stove. He got a cigar from the desk and lighted it but it had no taste.

Lot Yerington came in an hour later with some of the men who would eat and go back to relieve the others for the same purpose. A close watch would have to be kept on everything through the next crucial weeks; discommoding and wearing on the crew, but Yerington was a first-rate manager. The new arrivals vanished into the cookshack and after a while the foreman came into the office.

"It went all right again," he said. "Maybe we're goin' to be lucky."

Sperling looked doubtful. "I don't have much hope

they'll move their property out by night. It'll take fighting to burn 'em out. The easy going's over."

"Well," Yerington said confidently, "we've got the men for that, too. They've been a drain on the payroll so far. Now they can earn their money."

"Better sleep the boys in shifts today and have 'em all ready for night."

"Sure." The foreman went out.

Sperling made himself square up to a matter he had avoided even in the secrecy of his thoughts. It had grown on him in the way a man might watch a malignancy form in his body, hoping it would check itself naturally or turn out to be harmless. This was the matter of Penny's private interest in the nesters she championed: Cash Donovan.

Sperling knew they had met at the dances held in Broken Rock to relieve the monotony of the long, fierce winters. At first he had been pleased to have Penny attend them, for life on a ranch was dull for a woman without a husband and children to occupy her time. He had learned the winter before that she spent most of her time at those affairs with young Donovan. Now that was not enough of him to satisfy her, and she saw him surreptitiously in the basin, even going to his place. He no more questioned her morals than he would have doubted her mother's or his wife's. No, much more than that was involved.

The thought of her marrying a nester was intolerable in itself. If it was a nester fouling Dollarmark's range it became maddening. He told himself again that it was better to hurt her now, quick and sharp, than to let her be worn out by the life she would lead as the wife of a hardscrabble loner. She would inherit his property in a few years, and it was equally unacceptable to think of Donovan elevating himself to Dollarmark's management by becoming a foolish girl's husband.

The heat had soaked into him finally and Sperling drowsed in his chair. He roused with a start when somebody opened the office door which always complained on its hinges. His vision cleared to show him Buck Gillidge. He scowled for the old rider had left the ranch in heated disagreement with its policies, and Gillidge did not look friendly.

"Well, Hock," he said, mildly enough, "I see you're still bent on bloodshed."

"Who invited you here?" Sperling returned.

"I did. I seen them Dollarmark steers on the plateau and talked to one of your punchers. Them nesters ain't going to knuckle down to you, Hock, now or ever. You go over to burn 'em out and you'll be the one who's singed. There ain't much chance, but I hoped I just might make you believe it."

"I can stand the heat, Buck," Sperling said. "You ought to know it. The same as I stand cold and dry and anything else this country asks of a fellow. I opened it, I own it, and I'm not throwing in the sponge to any two-bit nesters."

"Then God pity you," Gillidge said. "Nobody down here's going to." He turned back toward the door.

Chapter 6

JEB PUZZLED for a moment over what had wakened him, trying to catch the sound again and locate and interpret it. The wind had died in the night but cold filled the room and all he could hear was the argument of the creek with its rocky bed. Reaching to the box that served as a bedstand he found a match and struck it. The clock on the table across showed him it was 5:30, about an hour away from daybreak at this time of year.

Cash said from his bunk, "You awake, too? What's the matter?"

"Dunno. What's the matter with you?"

"Thought I heard steers bawl." Cash sat up. "Hoped I dreamed it, but if you woke up, too, maybe I didn't."

Jeb swung his legs over the bunk. He struck another match, walked across and lighted the lamp on the table. The fire was clear out. Cash had got up and started to dress. Jeb's teeth began to chatter as he followed suit.

"Think Sperling's bringing steers in?" Cash asked.

"We better find out."

They finished dressing and strapped on their guns. Cash stepped to the door, opened it, and a voice rang out of the darkness.

"Stand still."

Two men slid into the room. They were Dollarmark riders and they gripped guns and grimness glazed their cold-tightened faces. They had been watching the house, Jeb realized. The light had told them that somebody had been aroused, so they had moved in to take over. With the door standing open, Jeb could hear the sound of distant cattle again, far out in the night, and knew that something was under way out there.

"You misbegotten sons," Cash said bitterly. "What're you up to now?"

"Take their hoglegs, Fitz," one said and the other stepped in to comply. "You boys go easy and you won't get hurt."

"What's going on?" Cash insisted.

The man still ignored him. "Walk over to that bunk and set down, you two. Fitz, you start a fire. We could sure use some heat."

Jeb seated himself on a bunk, Cash dropping down beside him, both dangerously on edge and furious. Fitz laid kindling in the stove. His companion took a chair, positioned so he could watch the prisoners.

"Hurry with that fire," he said. "It's been a cold night."

"Hands're like snowballs," Fitz grumbled.

"How long've you been out there?" Jeb said.

"Since midnight."

"Whats' going on?"

"Since you're so anxious for bad news, them's Dollarmarks comin' in."

"Where they going?"

"Onto this range. Where else?"

Jeb shook his head. "Better be somewhere else, buck. This range is too crowded."

"The nester stuff aint' there no more, anyhow."

Cash glanced at Jeb, deeply worried. He said nothing. Fitz got a fire started and went out to bring water for

45

coffee. The outer darkness had begun to thin. Later Lot Yerington rode up to the Battle Creek ranch house. To Jeb's surprise he only called the two punchers out and took them away with him. The whole outfit seemed anxious to avoid trouble, and it was easy to see why. Sperling was going far out on a limb without adding unneeded violence.

Once they were alone Cash surged to his feet, saying, "We'll see about this now."

"Simmer down," Jeb said calmly. "They've got a big advantage in numbers, and we've seen what they can do with it. Let's get something to eat, then see what we're up against and what we can do." It was a hard thing even for him to accept, yet it was an accomplished fact. "Lettin' off steam'd make us feel better, but it might hurt more than help."

They fell to work and made a hasty breakfast. Afterward they saddled horses and rode out to see what had happened to the other nesters on the plateau side of the mountains. Teebo had just reached Jorgan's place when they arrived at the Sagehen ranch. They had both been caught flatfooted, too. Dollarmark cattle thickly filled the nester valleys. Most of Sperling's crew was on hand to see that they weren't molested.

"See what I mean?" Jeb said to Cash, who nodded somberly.

"Looks like I'm the only one," Jorgan said, "Hock honored with a personal visit. He left it to me to deliver the message. If we ain't moved the rest of our stuff off the plateau by night, he said, they'll burn it, buildings and all. If we've minded him real nice, he'll buy the buildings."

"Did he say what happened to our cattle?" Cash asked.

"No, but you can bet they're scattered from here to breakfast. The first question is what to do about that deadline."

"They won't surprise us again," Cash said explosively. "Let 'em try to burn us out. This time we'll be set for 'em."

"You reckon the same thing happened on Muleshoe?" Teebo asked.

46

"Might as well go over and see," Jorgan said. "Not much left here we could lose, I guess."

Half an hour later they were well along the road that followed the foot of Dogleg. They had passed Battle Creek and a little later Cash said, "They're guardin' the pass." Two Dollarmark riders were in evidence down by the gap. They had a campfire and tent and seemed fixed for a long residence. "Let's warm things up a mite more for 'em."

"I wouldn't till we know why they're there," Jeb said. "Must be another way for us to get over the mountain to the mesa."

Jorgan, older than Cash and Teebo, shared Jeb's desire to know what he was tackling before he tied into it. He led the way onto Dogleg, across a little high valley, then down onto Head Creek at the upper end of Muleshoe. Presently they rode in to Trace Getty's shack. Getty wasn't home. The men from the plateau exchanged worried glances, fearing trouble had hit here also, but nobody said anything.

Riding farther down the mesa they discovered what had happened to the nester cattle. Plateau brands greatly outnumbered Getty's stuff and were scattered as far as the eye could follow, hopelessly entangled already with every brand there already.

"He wants this range, too," Cash said. "What's his caper?"

"Better find out what happened to the men over here," Jorgan said, his voice strained and worried.

There was no one at Jimmy Hooker's on the east fork of Mesa Creek. Plateau cattle were still in evidence. The riders struck across the mesa toward the creek's west fork where Buff Corey was situated at the foot of the Sapphires. Getty and Hooker were there with Corey and his three strapping sons. They had seen no one, they reported. The first they knew of the flood of plateau cattle pouring in on them was when they got up that morning and saw it all around them. It was the first time Jeb had seen Corey, who was an enormous man, full-bearded and shaggy-haired. His sons, Matt, Mark and Luke, were younger duplicates and there was no woman in evidence.

47

"You reckon Sperling's decided to settle for the plateau," Cash said, "and try and hold us here across the mountain?"

"If I know Sperling," Jeb said, shaking his head, "he's not giving up an inch of the old Dollarmark. Moreover, I don't think he'll let all these steers feed on mesa grass very long, either. He'll need that for his own stuff. What do you make of it, Getty?"

"I think you're right." Like the others, Getty was bewildered by the overwhelming superiority Sperling had demonstrated. Anger tightened his eyes. "But he ain't got it made yet, not by a long sight."

"It was gonna be a shoo-in," Cash said testily. "All we had to do was stand Sperling off till his steers ate him desperate and brung him to time for us."

The temper brightened in Getty's eyes. "We ain't licked yet."

"You don't know half of it yet. If we don't move off our spreads completely by dark we get burned out. Then what have we got to move back to? No steers, no layout."

"Simmer down," Jeb said.

"That's what I say," Getty said, though still rankled. "We ain't gonna fight 'em off tonight and day by day afterwards. We can't, and we don't have to. We're gonna make it plain that if a torch is laid to one of our buildings, Sperling'll get hit in the breadbasket. Namely, his own headquarters. That'll persuade him to keep some of his tough hands home. We can handle the rest."

"That sounds sensible," Corey said, "but meanwhile them plateau steers is raisin' cain with our own winter feed."

"One thing at a time. We'll check his threat to burn the plateau boys out. Then we'll get the Dollarmarks off the plateau and this mixed herd unscrambled."

"Might work," Cash said, encouraged and mollified. The others nodded.

"How about you, Jeb?" Getty said.

"Ready to burn Dollarmark if he calls you on it?"

"We sure are."

"Then it looks like you've got it figured."

48

Jimmy Hooker's straw-yellow hair stuck out wildly under his limp hat but his chilly face and eyes discouraged any impulse to be amused by that. He said, "Who warns Sperling?"

"I'll take that pleasure," Getty said. "The rest of you set tight till I get back."

"They've got men on the pass," Jorgan warned.

"I'll go over the Sapphires from here." Getty swung across his horse and rode out, for there was no time to lose. Presently the foothills swallowed him.

"Can't look for him back before noon," Corey said with a shake of his shaggy head. "Come on inside, boys, and warm up."

"While we're waiting," Jeb said, "I'd like to do a little poking around."

"Want company?" Cash asked. He was restless, still craving action and there was too much chance of coming upon a situation where he might crowd it. Jeb shook his head.

"You better be on hand when Getty gets back. I only want a look at what they've got on the plateau." He rode out toward the gap which he bypassed by going over the end of Dogleg as before, his mind on the enormous crisis confronting them.

Getty's strategy and present tactics seemed sound enough but would be more certain of success if Sperling hadn't added so many unscrupulous adventurers to his payroll. The pair that pinned them down that morning at Battle Creek had been from Sperling's older crew and had struck him as no better or worse than countless other punchers fighting for their outfits. The explosive, underhanded element was men like Trig Godfrey and Alf Heater or whoever had drygulched Tom. The nester cause wouldn't be hurt a bit if some of that bunch was eliminated and he had a strong personal wish to do so.

He angled off the lower Dogleg and came on Battle. From the distance the little P-D headquarters looked deserted, yet as he came nearer he observed a horse at the house. Presently he recognized Buck Gillidge who sat on the doorstep pulling on a pipe and staring moodily toward Jeb as he rode in.

"Howdy, Buck," Jeb said. "Out exercisin' your saddle muscles?"

Grumpily, Gillidge said, "I don't like what I'm out on a goldurned bit. It looks like things've been poppin' out here."

"They livened up some," Jeb agreed. "You had a look at the situation."

"Seen enough to know what's happenin'," the old man said. "I went over to talk sense into Hock Sperling. He wouldn't listen a minute. Which makes two things certain as sunrise and sin. The nesters'll defy him, and he'll burn 'em out and likely kill a few men in the bargain."

"Maybe not."

"Why not?"

"Trace Getty went over to warn Sperling Dollarmark'll burn to the ground if one of us does."

Gillidge shook his head. "Hock's a hard man to bluff."

"It's no bluff." Jeb sat down beside Gillidge on the step and started a cigarette. "Tell me something, Buck. Were Godfrey and Heater working for Dollarmark at the time you quit?"

"They were two of the reasons why I quit." Gillidge glanced at him shrewdly. "Why'd you ask that?"

"I think one or the other killed Tom. Either one a heavy smoker?"

"Well, Godfrey burns his share of the weed. Heater chews."

"That lets Heater out. You didn't happen to see Godfrey in town right after Tom was killed, did you?"

Gillidge shook his head. "Don't recollect it. I mark that day, too. Don't think I saw a soul from Dollarmark. Why?"

"Just a flimsy notion I had. Barking up the wrong tree, I guess." Jeb shrugged, disappointed. He was no closer to Tom's murderer than he had ever been.

Gillidge got to his feet, then looked down at Jeb. "You know what I'd do about Getty's warning if I was Hock? I'd hire me more men. When I could protect my own property I'd still carry the fight to the nesters."

"What'd you do if you were in Getty's boots leading the nesters?"

"Mebbe different to him."

Jeb stood up and looked at the old man's eyes a moment, his interest stirred deeply by the remark. "That's not very exact, oldtimer."

"You never trailed cattle the way we did in the old days, weeks and months on the road. The critters'd run all year without seein' a man or horse and they were some sudden in their notions once they were gathered in a bunch. Every outfit had a trained old mossyhorn to lead 'em to the railroad. Called 'em Judas steers. They were only dumb beasts, but I never could like one of the cusses. They were leadin' their own kind down the road to the slaughter house. And a man don't have a critter's excuse."

"You mean we've got a traitor?"

"I never said so. But was I you, I'd watch to see Trace Getty don't get the other nesters poleaxed."

"What makes you say that?" Jeb said. He had felt that way, Tom had, and now Buck.

"What I know about him. Getty never turned nester to slave and starve and beat his brains out for nothin' but bacon and beans. It ain't like him."

"You've got more reason than that," Jeb insisted.

"Sure have, and since you're a man who could handle him, I'm gonna tell you." Gillidge tapped the dottle out of his pipe. "Getty was gone from here a few years, rattling around in Arizona and New Mexico and on south of the border. Not many know it but he done time down there. He'd be doin' it yet, if he hadn't squealed on the gang he run with to get off easier. You'd call that the act of a traitor, I'd say, and I'd never trust him in any way again."

"Where'd you learn that?" Jeb asked.

"Found out one time when I went down to fetch in a herd for Hock. I never spread it because he's got a half-sister in Broken Rock."

"I met her and she struck me as a mighty fine girl who thinks highly of him."

"Only because she has no idea what he is."

"Maybe he's changed, straightened up."

Gillidge snorted. "You're a better judge of men than that. He let one bunch down, at least. I've got a idea

51

that this time he's out for somethin' that's to come at the others' expense."

"Well, thanks for telling me."

"Just hope you can handle him."

Chapter 7

GILLIDGE RODE west and Jeb swung onto his horse, his mind heavy with the information the old man had conveyed. Instead of making headway with his one puzzle, he had been confronted by another and now had to find out what Getty was really up to in the mounting range feud. His nagging feeling about the man had been right, apparently. It struck him that the puzzles might not be separate at all. Had Tom caught onto the man somehow and by what he said or did about it endangered his own life?

Bending south he rode onto the hump between Sperling and Battle Creeks and followed through its rocky juniper cover. He halted where he could see a sweep of the Battle Creek range, heavily dotted with Dollarmark cattle. He counted five men in view, loose-herding the stuff until the situation had stabilized. They made Getty's threat to throw the invaders off the plateau as the next step sound pretty vainglorious.

Jeb struck boldly down into Sperling Basin and came to the creek road. He followed this east and left it before he reached a point where he could be seen by the guards on the big gap. Afterward he struck into the Sapphires, began to climb and in about an hour reached a ridge trail and rode southward through the pines. The timbered land on his right fell away to the basin but on the other side flung up to a sharp, rocky spine.

He traveled for a number of miles, getting a good look at the section. There were only two passes beside the main gap by which cattle could be crossed from the basin to the mesa. Satisfied, he took the last pass and rode over and down onto Muleshoe. He came out on its extreme south end and swung back toward Buff Corey's.

Getty had come over the West Fork pass directly behind Corey's house and was there ahead of him. As he rode into the ranchyard Jeb noticed the lightened spirits of the nesters gathered about Getty. Cash grinned cheerfully at Jeb, indicating that he expected to get his action. Maybe Sperling had called Getty's hand and they had to carry out their threat.

"You get around," Cash called. "Disappear one way and pop up in another."

Jeb rode up to them and stepped out of the saddle. Turning to Getty, he said, "Get anywhere with Sperling?"

Getty nodded. "It just never occurred to the old boy we'd have the brains and gall to carry the fight onto Dollarmark itself if he keeps pushing us. But he knows it now."

"He call you or cancel the deadline?"

"Neither, but he won't be in a hurry to burn us out."

Jeb knew he had to lock horns with the man to determine how rigid Getty was in his course, for that might hint at his hidden objective. "Not till he's hired enough men to guard his own works, too. Which he will, then look out."

Getty frowned. "By the time he does that, we'll have his steers off the plateau, and there'll be no use burnin' us out."

"Getting his steers off the plateau is a tall order. I just counted five men on Battle Creek and there's probably as many on Sagehen and Squaw."

Getty glanced at him suspiciously, sensing that he was being baited. He seemed to take it as a bid for leadership and his shoulders stiffened. He said roughly, "Thought you were supposed to be a wild gun. You sound as leery as Tom."

Jeb checked his anger, for this made twice that Getty had betrayed a resentment of Tom. Quietly he said, "Let's leave personalities out of it, Getty. All ten of us couldn't knock 'em out of there, let alone move the cattle off. He's got even more men in reserve, and in trying it we'd leave the mesa here undefended. He could pull the same stunt on it while we were over there getting ourselves shot up."

"You got a suggestion?"

"Yes. Let's play it smart. Your overall plan is good. The other side of the mountain is still overstocked. Sperling's got to put some of their stuff on this mesa before real winter sets in. There's the main gap and two high passes he could bring 'em over. We can hold them. And you keep sayin' yourself winter's the thing that'll really lick him."

Getty's countenance grew darker, and his eyes held a disturbing light. Jeb scanned the other men, hoping they realized he had offered a plan to gain the same end without the ruinous risks but the stubbornness of their faces told him they weren't going to do it. Getty had them firmly under control, and he wasn't letting anybody else edge in on him.

"It won't work," Getty said with resumed confidence. "Sperling's grazing off grass we'll need ourselves before spring. He's got to be shoved out of there pronto."

"Then how do you aim to shove him?"

"We were talking that over when you showed up. Tonight Sperling's gonna be thinkin' about the deadline he gave us and the warning I gave him. So we do somethin' he ain't expecting."

"Like hitting the plateau?"

"That's the caper. The plateau boys'll go home and act like they're fixin' to fight off an attack tonight. After dark they'll slip out and meet the six of us from Muleshoe up Squaw Creek from Leet's place. We'll go down the plateau north of them and hit the Squaw bunch on the flank. The shootin'll help stampede the steers, which is the main idea."

"Pretty rough going in that direction," Jeb said, hoping to force more out of Getty. "There's breaks between every creek. The steers might run and again they might not."

"I think they will. We'll be on their flank and they'll try to get away from us. The farther we can move 'em the more the thing'll snowball, and it's sure worth tryin'."

Getty was discounting the obstacles and ignoring the imponderables, but the nesters were solidly behind him. He had a naturally positive personality, and maybe that

54

was the size of it, but he was surely bent on running things his own way. One indication stood out pretty plain in it. He no longer seemed content to stall Sperling and stand him off until he had to give up his ambitions. It could be a new idea or an old one previously hidden, but he seemed more than ready now to turn the tide against Sperling and overwhelm him. There could be a lot more profit in a drive like that for the man Buck Gillidge had described.

"You siding us, Jeb?" Teebo said.

"I don't think you can cut it, but majority rules. I'll do all I can."

Getty's eyes showed a curious satisfaction at that.

The plateau men left for home by the devious route they had taken coming over. Cash and Jeb peeled off at Battle Creek and rode down to the house. It was still deserted and unmolested. They put their horses in the corral, went in and built a fire.

"What makes you so leery of it?" Cash said finally.

Jeb shrugged. He had been debating whether to tell Cash what he had learned about Getty. "I feel what you told me once that Tom did. Getty might lead us into ruin if we let him. I ran into Buck Gillidge on my *pasear* today. He's got the same opinion of friend Trace."

"Old Buck?" Cash said with a snort. "He would have. His heart's still with Dollarmark, even if he did quit it. That was over Sperling's ways, not his purpose. What was in his craw?"

"He don't trust Getty."

Cash made a wry face. "And don't want you or me or the other nesters to. It'd help Dollarmark plenty if we all got real distrustful of Trace Getty about now. And that's what Buck was up to."

Jeb couldn't dismiss the possibility that Gillidge had acted out of such a motive. He didn't think so, considering his own instincts, but that was how Cash and the other nesters would see it.

They fixed a meal together, but Jeb knew a gulf had developed. When they had eaten Cash went showily about the business of preparing for an attack on the buildings. He sat on the doorstep and let some possible

Dollarmark spy see him clean his rifle. He brought in water and wood and turned the horses out in the pasture. Jeb knew the same ostentatious preparations were being made at the Squaw and Sagehen ranches to create the impression that the nesters were digging in for a fight at their headquarters. The die was cast and, though he would do his utmost to help bring the thing off, a sense of foreboding stayed with him.

When night came down fully they slipped back to the pasture and caught up their mounts again. Afterward they rode along the creek onto the mountain. The night was brightly cold with sharp stars hanging in clusters across the sky. A north wind blew from the high divide toward Idaho and tossed the juniper on the lower reaches of Dogleg. Swede Jorgan waited for them at the head of the Sagehen, and they rode on to Squaw. Teebo was there, dismounted and stomping his feet. In a matter of minutes the mesa party came down from the higher mountain. Some of them were armed with pistols and rifles both, and all were silent.

They meant to launch the assault in Teebo's valley, the Squaw. There were six Dollarmark men with that herd, Teebo reported, patrolling in pairs. That scattered them considerably. Getty held a match to a cigarette he had just rolled, his hands cupping the flame. He exhaled, nodding his head.

"It'll be like shootin' fish in a barrel," he said. "We'll sneak down the plateau and get into place and time it so we catch a couple on the far side of the steers. Let's ride."

They stayed on the mountain slope, using its cover, until they were at the juncture of a low range of hills spurring off toward the river. On north, Dogleg came in to abutt the river's sharp bend and the connecting level ground was narrower than it was farther down. Opposite Dogleg the range was contained by Sperling's line fence, which gave them a chance to drive the cattle down a broad slot aimed at Sperling Basin. This was what excited the nesters and gave them an overweening confidence in Getty's plan.

They moved behind the hills, ten silent men, until they reached a divide where they bent in to the edge of the creek valley. Halted in cover, Getty pulled out makings and rolled another cigarette although it was a dangerous place to strike a match.

"You hit those things pretty heavy," Jeb said.

"When I'm keyed up I eat 'em."

Something snapped in Jeb's mind like a steel trap. A heavy smoker had bushwhacked Tom—Getty had been in Broken Rock right after Tom was killed—he had a past that might destroy his leadership if it was revealed and believed by the nesters—Tom had distrusted him—he still disliked Tom. . . . Jeb saw in a flash that no one on Dollarmark was the personal enemy he had been seeking.

He could wait no longer, for some of these men who were trusting Getty so blindly would be dead in another hour. "Boys," he said raggedly, "there's too much you don't know about this fellow to follow him on a deadly long shot."

A volley fired at them out of the night would have caused no more consternation. Even the horses stirred as their riders swung to stare at Jeb. The starshine showed him their shocked and resenting disbelief.

"You sure seem determined to keep us off Sperling's back," Teebo said in a dangerous voice. "What are you talkin' about this time?"

"I'm telling you this much. I wouldn't trust my life to Trace Getty. It's not his judgment I'm questioning now but his real intentions, whatever they are, in using you in a wild effort to corner Hock Sperling. Corner, I say, because he turned down a far better plan to hold onto the range you claim."

"What do you base that on?" Jorgan said derisively.

"That's a good question." Getty's voice was charged with fury. "Supposin' you come up with a real good answer and real quick."

"I'll come up with another question. When did Tom find out you went over the road in Arizona and sold out the gang you run with to get off easier yourself?" That was all Jeb intended to reveal now. His suspicions as to who killed Tom and why were only suspicions, and a personal thing between him and Getty. "A traitor once

57

could be a traitor twice, and you're runnin' things too much your own way, Getty."

Getty's breath whistled on his teeth. "Where'd you pick up all that?" he demanded harshly. "Or are you makin' it up for some secret reason of your own."

"I'll tell you where," Cash said, as angry as the rest. "He seen Buck Gillidge and Buck slipped him a dose of pure poison, which he swallowed. Sperling put Buck up to it, you can bet your bottom dollar. They're tryin' to start a civil war over here for their benefit."

"You sure were a sucker," Corey agreed. "Old Buck rode for Sperling for years. When they fell out it wasn't over whether us nesters should be left alone. Buck's got the same old-fangled notions Hock has about that."

Jeb knew he had lost, just as Getty recognized his own triumph. The Head Creek nester stared across the fire-light with glittering eyes. The failure presented a choice that went badly against the grain. He had feared that disaster lay immediately ahead and had tried to prevent it. Now he had to eat crow or lose all contact with the man he had to expose and punish.

"Maybe I bought a bill of goods," he said.

"We'll take it for that this once." Getty clipped out the words. "And we've wasted too much time already, boys. Come on."

Ten strong aginst three or four times that number they moved down through the trees and brush skirting the low hills. Jeb went along, feeling a turbulent impotence. Getty dropped him off first. Off across the valley Jeb saw two riders moving beyond the cattle, indistinct blurs in the starlight. Down on the near right a couple of others were drawing near the line fence where they would have to swing south and farther away from the stalking nesters. Getty got his men all spaced out and they charged from cover in a long skirmish line, yelling and splitting the night with the sharp crackle of guns.

All over the valley frightened cattle sprang to their feet. Those already up hauled around to have a look at the onslaught of demons. They whipped again and went scampering off in the other direction, their alarm charging the whole herd. Jeb heard the beehive sound of rushing massed hoofs. Nesters cut to and fro, hostile shots rang out across the valley, but a stampede was under way.

Chapter 8

WILD AS they were, the cattle were not going to tackle the rocky brush along Squaw Creek ahead of them. Jeb saw a point shape itself on the up-valley side of the streaking mass. They would turn toward Dogleg Mountain, leaving the valley slot that would carry them into the basin, turning them deeper onto nester-claimed range. Two Dollarmark riders appeared out of the night and new gunfire streaked the dusty darkness. Other Sperling men would boil in from the farther valleys, turning bright hope into bitter disaster for the nesters.

Jeb put this swiftly through his mind, seeking a way to offset it. There was an open reach of creek a short distance upstream, to his left. If he could move fast enough, he might head the point toward it and turn the steers across. If kept in the valleys, as hoped for, the onslaught of cattle would tie up the Dollarmark men and keep them from mangling the nesters. Someone below him saw his intention and took up the idea. Jeb cut in on the racing leaders. He sent shot after shot ahead of them, yelling like a charging Piute. The other man did the same.

They risked being cut to ribbons by the maddened herd but together slanted its point toward the creek. The banks were gentle and the first steers swept down, went splashing across and out into the upper end of the Sagehen's valley. There they turned west where more room was evident. Jeb saw in relief that the crossers were towing the rest of the herd behind them, but the breaks between Sagehen and Battle were more rugged.

He sat his place and saw through the pale light that one of Buff Corey's boys had helped him head the animals. He could still hear shooting down the valley with no idea if it was fighting or aimed to keep the steers excited and going. Another rider appeared from the dust, coming toward them. When he saw yet another and realized he would no longer be needed at the crossing, Jeb rode on across the creek. He saw that the steers boiling in had alarmed the cattle bedded down in this section. They were all milling madly, contained by the tumult on one side and the forbidding breaks on the other.

What he saw when he looked in the other direction brought him stiff-legged on the stirrups. A large party of horsemen was whipping in from the head of the valley. They were more Sperling men who apparently had been moving in on the nester headquarters to enforce the deadline when this commotion started. They could still save their pent-up cattle by beating off the harassers. He swung his horse around and went driving back across the creek.

"Dollarmark!" he shouted as he approached the nesters at the crossing. "And too many of 'em! Pull back into the dust!"

They were Teebo, Hooker and Luke Corey, he saw. Their disbelief was shattered when guns across the creek cracked open the night and lead sought them in dead earnest. The oncomers had seen and bent toward him as he crossed back.

Momentarily they were willing to take his advice. Jeb rode after them into the dust along the edge of the streaming cattle. He hoped they had vanished unseen, otherwise there might not be a live nester left by morning. They came upon Swede Jorgan, then Matt Corey and took them in tow. They found the others in the rear of the herd, still harrying the cattle.

"Dollarmark comin'!" Teebo yelled. "Scads of 'em!"

Getty gave him a hard stare. "Which way?"

"Up the crick!"

"We'll give 'em a charge!" Getty's voice was high-pitched with excitement.

"Dunno, Trace," Corey said uneasily.

"Me, neither," Hooker added. "The steers ain't behavin' at all like we figured, and a big part of Dollarmark is free to fight. No use throwin' our lives away for something that won't work nohow."

It was the first time Getty had encountered rebellion

60

in his own backers. He flung Jeb a hard stare, clearly holding him responsible. He was impressed enough to avoid a showdown on the spot. But he tried to let himself down easy.

"We been blind as bats back here. What's happenin' across the crick?"

"They're only millin' and it's ten to one they'll run down."

"All right, let's get."

They had already wasted too much time. Horses emerged in the thin dust and the rattle of guns came rollicking through the choking mantle. The nesters returned the fire but they were well sobered by then. Speedily they pulled off toward the hills from which they had emerged to start the action. Dollarmark came after them in full cry.

Jeb saw that their only chance to survive was to split up, every man for himself. He yelled at the others, who seemed to agree with him for the second time that night. They fanned out, driving for the hills where they had a chance to lose themselves. Bullets riddled the night about them, and they fired back to slow down the pursuit. The scattering had the effect Jeb hoped for. It broke Dollarmark into separate parties and drew them well apart also.

When he emerged from the dust hanging over the valley Jeb whipped his horse around, ready to take advantage of the moment when any followers appeared out of the obscurity behind. None did so, although he heard hot firing to his right and left. He pressed into a draw, emerged on the back side of the spur and stopped again. He still wasn't followed.

It took twenty minutes for the bulk of the nester party, which had started out so confidently, to straggle in. It had grown evident by then that Dollarmark was satisfied to drive them away from the cattle. They were all there finally but Luke Corey and Cash Donovan.

"They must've come out farther east," Luke's father said worriedly.

They rode in that direction for a couple of miles without finding the two missing men. But there had been no agreement to congregate outside the hills, and it was possible that Luke and Cash had headed on already for

61

safer ground. Yet the two weren't at Teebo's place nor at Jorgan's.

"Somethin' happened to 'em," Corey said tersely. "I'm goin' back."

"I'll come along," Jeb said.

They returned down the outer side of the hills and threaded a draw to find that the dust had pretty well settled in the valley. "There's a horse," Corey said gruffly. "And a empty saddle. But it don't look like the critter Luke was ridin'."

They couldn't tell very much from the distance. The animal stood off to the left, trying to graze, indifferent to the violence that had so recently surrounded it. Having cleared the valley, the large Dollarmark party seemed to have ridden over to the Sagehen to help handle the aroused cattle.

As they rode nearer to the horse, Jeb's heart contracted. Cash had been in that saddle when the rout started. He rode in and caught the horse by the reins, Corey close behind him. They struck out on a line toward the point where the nesters had broken up. About half way they found Cash, on the ground, unmoving. Jeb sprang from the saddle, not daring to breathe until he discovered the faint pulse in Cash's wrist. Even in the thin light he could see the blood that had run out from under the wounded man.

Bitterly Corey said, "That's two of our'n now."

"Cash's still alive."

"I wonder what happened to Luke, though."

"He's still in the saddle or we'd see his horse, too. Could be he headed straight for the mesa from here. There was no arrangement about that. We better take care of Cash, then see."

"Can he stand movin'?"

"Have to."

"Where'll we go with him?"

That was a question to which Jeb had no quick answer. There was no security for a badly wounded man anywhere on the lateau. They were as close to town as to the mesa, and Cash could get better treatment there.

"Broken Rock," he said. "You go back for a couple more men. Throw together a litter and bring it back

62

with you." He saw the lingering fear in Corey and amended that. "Send some of the other boys. I reckon you want to find out about Luke."

Corey nodded and rode up the valley.

Jeb sat on his heels beside the wounded man, anger replacing his first shock. Whatever else he held against Getty he couldn't hold him responsible for starting the range feud. That was the sole fault of Hock Sperling, a man who had appropriated untold acres of the public domain. He had made a fortune from the land and now used intimidation and bloody violence to maintain his hold on it.

He waited a long while before Getty appeared with Teebo and Jorgan. They brought a blanket litter and crude materials for dressing Cash's wound, a torn gash in front and back of his right chest. They moved out for Broken Rock by way of the river road to avoid a chance encounter with Dollarmark again. The going was slow and they moved silently, each lost in his own thoughts. They were sobered thoughts now, Jeb knew, impassioned and bitter still but at last made doubtful of the ultimate outcome of the struggle. Dollarmark's claws were sharp and the power with which they struck was as yet too great for them.

At Getty's suggestion they took the wounded man to Anita's home. The windows were shaded but brightened by light beyond, and she hurried out at Getty's call. When she understood the meaning of the litter, she came running down the walk.

"What happened, Trace?" she gasped. "Who is it?"

"Cash Donovan," Getty said. "There was a rumpus and he's hit pretty hard. Thought you wouldn't mind having him here close to a doctor."

"Of course I wouldn't. He can have your old room. Bring him in."

In a matter of minutes Cash was transferred to a bed. Since he knew the town, Jorgan left on the double to bring the doctor. The other men undressed Cash and made him as comfortable as possible. All they could tell about his condition was that he was still breathing.

The doctor was there in another half hour and ordered everyone but Anita from the room. He would make no comment until he had examined the patient. Jeb went out to the kitchen with the three nesters. Getty seemed deeply disturbed by the turn of events and looked around uneasily at the others.

"Well, it didn't come off like we hoped," he said.

"Just the same, it was a darn good try," Teebo said encouragingly. "They know we ain't any pushovers, anyhow. It showed Sperling he'll get as good as he gives, every time."

It was clear they didn't hold Getty to blame, which relieved the man somewhat and helped repair his pride. "You made some awful rough charges, Jeb," he said bitterly. "We were all keyed up, and I'm trying to remember that, but it seems to me you were a sight too quick to swallow what old Buck told you."

"Since you bring it up, tell us something. Do you deny having a prison record?"

Jeb was as surprised as the other two listeners when Getty shook his head. "No. Since it's come up, I'd best admit that. But Gillidge took and twisted it all around, tryin' to benefit Hock Sperling. It was like this. I was off on a *pasear* for three or four years, and I sure tried to sow some wild oats. I run with a pretty wild bunch, and we got into trouble and went over the road. The reason I got off lighter was that I was only a kid at the time. Anybody who says I squealed on the others is lyin' in his teeth. How'd Buck know, anyhow? Did he locate and question all the others, or did he just hear some gossip? Or did he make it up to serve his stinkin' purpose?"

Jeb shrugged.

Angrily, Teebo said, "Well, you can't blame a man just sproutin' whiskers if he makes a misstep. Not if he learns his lesson."

"I sure learned mine," Getty said. "I come back figuring to cut out the nonsense and make something out of myself. That's why I set up on the mesa. It's why I'm ready to fight till they kill me for what I've built myself out there."

He knew that Jeb didn't believe him, and probably he didn't care. He had admitted the one thing that could be proved on him by the public record and the natural

64

charity of his followers was already working in his favor. He had chosen in this way to give himself the advantage over his accusers, avoiding an open contest by pretending honesty. Only the two of them would realize that thereafter a seething, insistent enmity would lie between them.

They all turned their heads. The doctor had appeared in the doorway, an aging man with a shock of iron grey hair, whom the nesters had called Sullivan.

"What's the outlook, Doc?" Jorgan said quickly.

"Well, it's a mean case. The slug come in from an angle and drilled a lung then glanced off the side of the spine."

"You—don't think he'll live?" Jeb said.

"I sure wouldn't bet on it. And if he does, he might be paralyzed. That depends on what damage was done to his spine."

Teebo swore under his breath.

"Do all you can," Jeb said. "I'm footin' the bill. If you can find one, get a town woman to come in and help Miss Toinbee."

The doctor nodded and went back.

"Looks like a long haul here," Getty said. "I reckon we'd as well get back and see what happened to Luke Corey."

"I'll hang around a while," Jeb said. The others seemed willing to dispense with his company and left.

Anita came out of the sick room and sat down across the table from him. "Doc Sullivan's done a little good," she said. "Cash is breathing better and his pulse is stronger."

"Mighty nice of you to let us impose on you."

She looked at him in surprise. "I wouldn't have it any other way. Wouldn't you like something to eat?"

"No grub, but if you don't mind I could stand some coffee."

She sprang to her feet and soon had a fire going in the kitchen range. She wore a plain dress, and though she had been busy helping the doctor her hair was still combed neatly. "You're pretty concerned about Cash, aren't you?" she said without turning around.

"Well, I took a liking to him."

"Doc Sullivan's one of the best, and I'm glad he wasn't in the country on a call." She batched coffee and set it forward on the stove top to cook. When she swung back she was frowning. "I caught snatches of what you men were saying out here, Jeb. Have you and Trace had trouble?"

He felt his heart give an extra kick. "I guess that's something you should ask him about, Anita."

"He's pretty impetuous," she said with a sigh. "Was he responsible for what happened tonight?"

"I wouldn't say so."

She gave it up but was troubleed, and he wondered how much she had overheard. Presently Sullivan came in. "He'll sleep quite a while now, Anita, and there isn't much to do but watch him. If he starts to hemorrhage from the mouth, though, call me quick."

"I will. You want some coffee?"

Sullivan shook his head. "Keeps me awake, and I get enough of that from people knocking on my door at night."

Anita saw him out the front way. When she came back Jeb said, "I hope it won't bother you if I stick around tonight."

"Not at all."

"And you might as well go to bed. I'll take care of Cash."

She regarded him, seemed about to object then changed her mind. She said, "All right," and left.

He drank more coffee, wondering how she could have so pleasant an effect on him when her half-brother was the exact opposite. He thought she liked him, too. But that would change rapidly when he and Trace Getty finally tangled, which could come now at any hour.

Chapter 9

JEB SPENT his time between Cash's room and kitchen, angry and worried, and day came with no apparent change in Cash's condition. Anita was up with the dawn and by then the bedroom in which the patient lay had a sick room's gloom and smell. Getty had been right in one thing. It would be a long haul for Cash, if he made it at all.

"Get some sleep, Jeb," she said quietly. "I can do him as much good as you can."

"I'll go to the hotel."

"There's no need of that," she said irritably. "But have some breakfast first. I'll have it ready in a minute." She was depressed, maybe because of the injured man, possibly because she had overheard enough last night to guess at the truth of many things previously hidden from her. Whatever disturbed her, it seemed to be something she didn't care ot discuss. Even diluted blood was thicker than water, and she had known and trusted Trace Getty a lot longer than she had known Jeb Pelton.

He stepped out to the back porch and washed his hot face. Night vapors still mantled the town, beading the grass and shrubs and frosting the window glass. The deepening cold cut through him. He combed his hair and grew aware of a horse scuffing along the street in front. It stopped before the house. When he stepped back indoors Anita was disappearing into the front of the house. He heard her exclaim, "Why, Penny!"

Jeb followed into the other room and saw the girl from Dollarmark hasten across the porch to the door Anita held open for her. She looked pale and dazed and beaten. In a voice tight with fear, she gasped, "The men said they brought Cash here, Anita. Is he—?" She couldn't complete the question.

"He's still alive, honey," Anita said gently.

"Thank God. I hope you don't mind this. I just had to come."

"Of course you did." Anita helped the stricken girl out of her coat and sent her to the fire. When she saw the restless way Penny looked about, she changed her mind. "He's unconscious yet. But I expect you'd like to see him a minute anyway before you warm up. He's in there."

Penny glanced at her gratefully then slipped into the bedroom, closing the door. "Well, what do you think of that?" Jeb murmured.

"I think it's the most natural thing in the world. They're in love, and heaven help them."

"Amen to that."

They went back to the kitchen where Anita served a quick breakfast. Before they had finished eating, Penny came out to join them. She was still pale but her face was composed again, resolute.

"What does the doctor think?" she asked quietly.

"He doesn't know, Penny," Jeb said. "How did you learn of it?"

"I knew something dreadful was happening last night," she said bitterly. "When my grandfather came home I made him tell me what it was."

"He knew Cash was hit?" Jeb said in surprise.

She shook her head. "I was worried about him and rode over to Battle Creek. I met the men who helped bring him to town and they told me. I came on and I'm not going back, ever. Will you let me stay here a while?"

"As long as you want, Penny," Anita said promptly. "If anybody can help Cash now, you can."

"He's got to live," Penny said fiercely. " He's got to help humble that old tyrant at Dollarmark."

Jeb glanced at her curiously, surprised at the change emotion had wrought in her. At their last meeting she had defended Hock Sperling.

Jeb left them together and went into the living room to smoke a cigarette and think. He wasn't going to be needed here and emotion had effected changes in himself as well as in Penny. The death of Tom had made him Cash's partner in legal fact if not in spirit. Now Cash's incapacity made the responsibility for the little spread his alone, and he felt it keenly. It had done more, enlisting him against Dollarmark with a vengeance he had not harbored until now.

When Penny went back in with the hurt man, Anita came over to Jeb. In a guarded voice, she said, "I heard Trace admit he was in prison. I gathered that you forced it out of him. Why?"

Stiffening, he said, "He's pretty well runnin' the nester side of the show, Anita, which makes a great deal hang on the kind of man he is."

"You don't believe he's reformed."

"I hope he has."

"Which is another way of saying you don't think so. I don't call that very fair. He's entitled to a new start. Everyone is."

"Nobody's denying that."

She looked away, deeply troubled, and was watching the empty street when she said, "I hoped we could be friends."

"We're not any more?"

"That depends. Trace is the same as a full brother to me. We grew up together. I have a feeling you're out to get him for some reason. I've sensed it ever since last night. Do you deny it?"

"No."

"Care to explain it?"

"I can't."

"You cared the most about Tom," she said fiercely. "I told you that day that Trace was the only one from out there I saw in town right after he was killed. I hope I'm not the one who made you suspicious of him."

"Only in part."

She turned and went back to the kitchen.

He waited until the doctor had made his morning visit, which did not brighten the outlook, then got his horse and rode out of Broken Rock. The air held a nipping chill as he crossed the river and struck the prairie road. Three hours later he rode in to the Battle Creek headquarters, half expecting to find them burned. They were intact. When he found Jorgan's place deserted also he decided that the nesters had returned to Muleshoe Mesa.

He slanted across Dogleg and came down on Head Creek to find Teebo and Jorgan at Getty's place. The owner was not in evidence and the plateau ranchers showed a mingled surprise and concern at his arrival.

"Nothing wrong, I hope," Jorgan said.

"Cash is holdin' on but that's all. Where's Getty?"

"Went down to Corey's."

"Luke turn up?"

Jorgan nodded. "The men that chased him hung on like burrs and he hit for the hills to shake 'em. But he's all right."

"What's Getty going to do next?"

"He ain't said much, except that me and Leet had better make his place our headquarters for a while. We've got to forget the plateau for the time being, take care of our stock and hold onto what we've got left. Then we can start on the comeback."

That was precisely what Jeb had recommended before the abortive sally against Dollarmark on the plateau, Jeb reflected, but all he said was, "That's once I agree with him."

Jorgan eyed him. "Well, now that he admitted there's some cause for your feelings, I can see your mind better. But you don't know him like we do, and you're dead wrong if you still think he ain't turned over a new leaf."

"You don't know how much I hope that, Swede."

Jeb rode on south along the foot of the Sapphires, heading for Buff Corey's. He arrived to find that Getty had gone over to Jimmy Hooker's ranch on the other side of the mesa. The three Corey boys were catching up on sleep but Buff was up. His first question was about Cash, who had been as popular with the nesters as Jeb knew himself to have grown unpopular.

"Where's Cash's cattle?" Jeb asked when he had reported on the wounded man.

Corey shook his head. "Everything's so scrambled it'll take a roundup to separate 'em, even to tell what's where."

"The mesa might have to carry the whole load a while," Jeb said. "Seems to me some smart herdin' would help. Some of the stuff could go farther out on the desert till the first real storm. Some might be put back on Dogleg a while longer."

"How can we spare the time for that?"

"If we fortified the passes, some of us could take care of the stock while the others stood guard against Sperling."

Corey scratched his fingers through his heavy beard. "That might not be a bad idea. Why dont' you talk to Trace about it?"

"Better chance of him adopting it if it sort of popped into mind as his own idea. You could manage that better than I could."

70

"I reckon you're right. Where you gonna be?"

"Reckon I'll rattle around a little."

He struck up the West Fork canyon behind Corey's place, heading for the pass. He was convinced that a strong defense of the mesa would come closer to bringing success than any amount of aggressive action against the big outfit. Time was on their side, and the deep winter would do more to Sperling than the nesters could ever manage, requiring no needless bloodletting. If Getty would settle for that there would be no apparent reason to distrust his motives in the struggle.

He reached the pass and confirmed his impression that it would be easy to fortify strongly. Abundant rock lay close at hand with which to block it completely if need be and a couple of men could defend the barrier as long as necessary. The same pattern would seal the pass farther south, and some modification could be found for the main gap, already guarded on the basin side by Sperling.

He had never taken a look at the southern half of Sperling Basin and he rode down that side of the mountain. This brought him out on a high rock rim several miles south of Dollarmark headquarters. He reined in and swung out of the saddle to warm his feet. Walking about, he stopped now and then to make a brief inspection of the country below him.

There seemed to be no more cattle in evidence than would be normal on any range, and this puzzled him. When his chilled fingers would work well enough to roll a cigarette he smoked, then he swung back across the horse. High ground had kept him from seeing far to the south, so he continued in that direction, the rocky rim still falling away below him.

He halted in quick, chilling understanding of why the range seemed so surprisingly uncrowded when there had been talk by the nesters to the contrary. Off there between the rim and the brush belt of a creek a herd as large as the plateau invaders had been gathered. Men were holding it where natural formations did not serve the same purpose.

Dollarmark was prepared to strike again, and this time the objective had to be Muleshoe Mesa. The only thing surprising was the speed with which Sperling had moved.

It looked doubtful now that there would be time to fortify the passes, to which Getty and the nesters would have to agree. There could be a repetition of what had happened on the plateau except that this time they would be warned and not caught flatfooted. An idea born of urgency shaped itself in his mind.

Swinging left, he rode across the narrow bench to the edge of the timber, which he penetrated. It took several minutes to find a rotting downfall that would provide dry tinder. He filled his hat with this and bark chips and went back to the open. Returning, he gathered an armful of dead branches. He kindled a blaze in the tinder, fed and built it up. He went into the woods again and cut an armload of green boughs. He wanted a lot of smoke.

He returned to his growing bonfire and stood beside it, warming himself while he waited. The day was still enough so that the growing smoke trailed away on the slanted vertical. Satisfied, he threw on the boughs. Leaving the horse where it was he slipped back to the rim, crawling in the last few feet to the edge where he could see.

They hadn't noticed the smoke yet but could not long avoid it. A heavy column curled and twisted as it climbed into the cold upper air. He saw three mounted men on the north of the herd. He counted a couple on the far end and there could be more, here to keep the cattle ready to move at a moment's notice.

He thought his plan had failed until at last a rider looked up toward him and sat through a breath in fixed staring. The distant figure pointed and seemed to call something to the others, who rode up to him, also looking up toward the boiling smoke. The excitement leaped across to the men visible beyond the herd. They could only surmise that a signal was being sent to the nesters on Muleshoe Mesa to warn of what was poised here, ready to threaten them again.

The punchers could not reach the rim top without riding up a trail and none was in sight. Jeb saw the closer men huddle and gesticulate, their horses wheeling nervously. Then one cut out on a dead run, driving toward headquarters. Jeb smiled grimly. He had succeeded in throwing the big outfit on the defensive, a condition that might gain the nesters a few hours to prepare themselves. He returned to his horse, swung across it and headed for the pass.

Chapter 10

HOCK SPERLING paced his office, striding from his battered old desk to the potbellied stove that pitted its heat against the blustery day outdoors. The night's tensions had left him too drawn and edgy to rest. On top of that had come his granddaughter's undisguised revulsion when he told her what he had done to the nesters. A little later, when he saw her ride out from Dollarmark, he had known she was going to see the young whipppersnapper who had got his loathesome hold on her young affections. Later, Lot had told him that Donovan had been wounded in the fighting and taken to Broken Rock, that Penny had earned of this and gone in to town herself.

A testy resentment of everything contributing to his troubles rode Sperling's sagged shoulders. It contained a galling element of humiliation. The girl had advertised her disloyalty to him and her sympathy for his enemies to the whole country, a country that in the beginning had belonged to him alone. She had become as strange to him as the new people along the Humboldt and the new ideas and weird assumptions they had brought with them. He had the feeling if he could not continue to rule his household, his last hope of holding his range was gone.

When he saw Trig Godfrey go by the window, he stepped to the door and opened it, calling, "Trig, tell Lorn to saddle my bay."

The puncher glanced at him, nodded and went on. Sperling walked briskly to the wall rack and lifted down his sheepskin, his sharp features set in a glacial mold. Donning the coat, he clapped on his old, high-crowned hat and stood grumpily by the window until the wrangler came up with his horse. Emerging, Sperling stepped across the horse and, without a word, rode out on the lane to the town road.

He had made this ride countless times and ordinarily it gave him satisfaction to travel mile after mile along a creek named for him, through a basin named for him, and on rangeland indisputably his own. No such feeling came to him now, and his resentment rose higher and centered on the wisp of a girl who had slipped beyond him and his grasp. She knew the pride in him and without hesitation had mocked it. He reached town shortly after noon, went into the Exchange for a drink to warm him and to make his veiled inquiries. When he learned that Donovan was at the Toinbee girl's place, he knew where to find Penny.

The dark girl, whom Sperling knew only by sight, responded to his rap on her door. She gave him a quick, uneasy study when she recognized him and seemed about to order him off in a sudden rise of temper when she reconsidered.

"You're here about Penny, of course," Anita said. "You wouldn't be concerned about the man you shot."

"I've come," Sperling said stiffly, "to fetch my granddaughter home."

She stepped back and shut the door, and Sperling wondered if it was to remain closed to him. Anger gusted through him, and he was about to lay a hand on the knob when the door opened again. Penny came through, pulling the panel to behind her, and Sperling experienced a slight uncertainty when he saw her eyes. They belonged to a stranger.

"This is no place for you," he said. "Where's your horse?"

"You're wrong," Penny said quietly. "Dollarmark's no place for me, anymore. I'm not going back there, and you'd best get used to the idea. Let's not have a scene about it, either. There's a man inside who might be dying. I don't know. But I do know that I love him and that you did it to him. I'll never be able to bear the thought of you and your pride of possession again."

The flat, even run of her voice told him the desolation within her, and the drive that had brought him here went completely out of Sperling. He had always considered her an extension of himself, and it came to him as a shock that she was a person within herself, one he had

74

never really known. That rendered his arguments useless.

Sperling said fiercely, "Then stay here and face the music along with the rest of them."

He turned, descended the steps and walked back to his waiting horse.

He reached Dollarmark to see Lot Yerington and a puncher riding in from the south side of the basin. He had just turned his horse over to the wrangler when he noticed them but was too lost in thought to wonder what hurried them. He traipsed back across the big yard to the welcome privacy of his office.

Still buttoned to the chin in his sheepskin, he crossed to his desk, withdrew a bottle of whiskey, uncorked and lifted it to his cold-blued lips. It was a dirty trick to be old, to have to fight the growing weaknesses of his body as well as to pit himself lonehanded against a hostile world.

Yerington's boots hit the plank outside the office. Sperling turned around just as the foreman came through the doorway, followed by one of the new punchers who called himself Art Sternberg.

"Well, the nesters caught onto the steers we been holding for Muleshoe Mesa," Yerington said tonelessly. "Seems to have occurred to 'em to watch the Sapphire passes, as well as the Gap. They're gonna do something about them steers, I think."

Sperling cleared the burning taste of raw Whiskey from his throat. "What do you mean?"

"Some nester sent a smoke signal to somebody from the rim."

Worry rammed through Sperling. Once he had seemed to have a magic touch that gave him confidence in all his undertakings. Too many things had gone too badly wrong, in the present effort, to let him feel that way now. Yet this brought him no uncertainty as to the necessities confronting him. Dollarmark had to move boldly, mercilessly, until it had regained its own.

Waiting patiently, Yerington said finally, "You want to go ahead tonight, anyhow?"

"Certainly," Sperling said waspishly. "Why would I do otherwise?"

"Everything depended on us surprising 'em again. If

they don't hit us before we get moving, they can cost us when we get to the pass."

"It can cost them, too, and we can afford it better." Sperling's voice rang with temper, which brought a ruddy color under the weathered brown of the foreman's face.

"They're your steers," Yerington said grumpily, and the pair went out.

The heat of the room and the stiff pull of whiskey had begun to tell. Sperling got out of his heavy coat and hung it up, clapping his hat on the same peg. Suddenly he felt vulnerable, almost whipped. Penny's renunciation had cut him more deeply than he had realized. Dollarmark seemed empty without her, to have no meaning if it was not to become hers when he was gone, along with the times for which he stood. Yet this stray thought was entirely intolerable. He had to die, as all men did, but it was not true that his era was dying. He and men like him were entitled to a longer tenure than one lifetime. With their work, wits and courage they had bought the right to pass it on. Those who threatened him had best get out of his way if they did not want to be destroyed. He had never been that merciless before, but the would be so from here on out.

He considered the nesters who were the spearhead of the class that wanted to take over the country. He thought little of Trace Getty, whom he had not liked even before Getty squatted on Head Creek. The others were men cut more to the pattern he appreciated, and the man who had thrown in with them—Jeb Pelton — had compelled him to a grudging respect. For all his fury, that day when Pelton rode in to Dollarmark so contemptuous of the odds against him, Sperling had been impressed. There used to be more men of Pelton's kind. His unyielding spirit was of the right sort, even if he had enlisted it on the wrong side.

With Donovan out of action, Sperling reflected, there would be nine nesters left to handle, a pitiful handful compared to the number now on Dollarmark's payroll. They might strike at the herd where it was, as Yerington feared, but they had tried that sort of thing on the plateau only to wish they had not. They were more apt to fight at the passes, he thought, where the odds would be better for them. Since there were three passes cattle could cross, they would have to guess the right one to defend or spread themselves cripplingly thin trying to cover them all.

But why had that smoke signal been sent up when it was as certain to be seen by Dollarmark men as by a nester on the summit? Had it been to confuse and throw the big outfit off stride? Pelton would be smart enough to pull a trick like that.

Sperling stayed away from the ranchhouse and its empty memories until night came down and cowhands drifted in from the range to fill the big yard with their noise and activity. Cold flowed in from the north to remind him that killing weather was not far away. Just before the cook belabored the triangular gong to announce supper, Yerington rode in from the held herd. There had been no trouble so far, he told Sperling, but he had doubled the guard and would be glad when the critters were established on Muleshoe.

Sperling ate with him in the cookshack, as he frequently did when they had something to talk over, and he was conscious of the way the men watched him covertly. They knew, of course, that his own flesh and blood had turned against him in favor of a nester. It was galling to feel the rake of their eyes and wonder if they joked among themselves about it. There was no loyalty anymore, not like there used to be. Nowadays, if a man had to defend his ranch he had to hire professional gunslingers, but it hadn't always been that way. Pride once was enough and the kind of spirit that held the oldtime outfits together.

Although he had known all along what he was going to tell Yerington, Sperling waited until they had finished eating and gone outside.

"I'm going to take some men up to Thimble Pass and probe it," he said then. "You'll set tight with the herd till I send word to bring 'em on."

"If you do," Yerington said moodily, "ten to one they've got men at all the passes. In a tight place like that they could raise hob with us."

"Getting scared of 'em, Lot?"

The foreman cursed softly. "You know better than

that. He had his share of courage, but it stopped at the point where the wanton sacrifice of good beef cattle began. He knew that this man was a fanatic, carried beyond reason by his feelings. Having set out to reclaim Muleshoe, too, Sperling would do it if he had only one steer left, when the dust settled, and one puncher left to herd it.

"Then quit spookin'," Sperling snapped. "I don't think they'll trouble the herd till it reaches the mesa. They're too shorthanded."

"How many men you want?"

"Give me half a dozen and include Heater and Godfrey. If the sons are up there on the summit, I want men with nerve."

"What time?"

"They'll look for it in the middle of the night, like the last time. This trip we'll make it early. Soon as you can get ready."

"That won't take long."

It was a few minutes after nine when Sperling rode out with his squad of tough cowhands, breasting into a stiffening wind under a dim full moon. They moved steadily southward and, since they might be watched, he led his men toward the shadowy footslope of the Sapphires where it rose to the West Fork pass. It was his notion that the nesters would watch Thimble, which was directly between the herd and Muleshoe. This maneuver might serve to concentrate them at the head of the West Fork instead. That was an incidental consideration, however. Mainly he hoped to slip up on Thimble Pass unobserved from the side.

His men rode silently, hunched against the cold and minding his orders against smoking until the job was done. They carried no loose equipment, and except for the padding footfalls of the horses they moved like phantoms through the bunchgrass and sage. It took an hour of such travel to carry them to the darkening timber that rose with the mountain. Sperling led them on into the deep shadows, relying on his timeworn memory to keep him on the trail. In about ten minutes they filed into an open plateau and swung right, not long afterward nearing Thimble Pass on its flank.

The mountain ridge broke in a narrow fracture between the heads of two descending creeks. There was over a mile of this before the canyons on either end debouched onto the timbered plateaus. Sperling had expected the near end to be manned but, as he rode up stealthily, he could see no sign of it. If there were nesters on hand, they were hidden in the abundant cover. It did not seem reasonable that they would maintain such cramped positions for hours, when a band of cattle could not come within a mile without warning them. He had hoped to catch them in the open, lulled by the fact that there had been no such notice, and either capture or drive them off.

"What you think?" Trig Godfrey, who had pulled up on his right, whispered excitedly. "They leave the gate open on purpose, or because they ain't got enough men to hold us back?"

Sperling lacked the answer to that, but one thing was clear. He could not surprise men he had not located. Nor could he send cattle into that narrow, rock-walled slot without being certain they would not be molested. An arrogant impatience rose in him, and he said, "One way to find out. We'll ride through the thing ourselves."

Godfrey gave him a quick look, and Sperling could feel the stares of the others reach and rake over him. But he had hired them for fighters and paid them as such, and he swung his horse to the right, slanting down-slope toward the trail that lifted directly into the canyon. He had put their pride to the test, and they followed, but he knew they disliked it. He was relieved, himself, when they entered the stricture without setting off an eruption of trouble.

Hoofs hit the flinty earth, and the sound rang back from the rock cliffs that soon rose with no discernible widening for nearly a hundred feet overhead. The riders came to the summit, which was marked by a rearing pinnacle more than a change in grade, and a moment later Sperling pulled down.

Directly below them a pile of rocks, brush and logs filled the canyon to the height of a mounted man's head and ran from wall to wall.

"Well, what do you know?" Alf Heater intoned. "They been busy little bees, ain't they?"

Sperling's lips compressed in anger. A lot of work had gone into building that barrier, with materials rolled down from on top, and it would take even more to remove it. The cattle could not pass over it. Even if he tore it down enough to slope off its sides, they would risk broken legs getting over. Nonetheless it was an opportunity, for the nesters were relying on it to hold Thimble while they concentrated their men at the two passes that could not be blocked in this manner. They did not think he could go through here, but if he could manage it he would accomplish his purpose in a way that would humiliate as well as defeat them.

"Clear out the center," he said roughly. "Make a path wide enough for the critters to go through double file."

Men of their breed disliked hard work, but his riders saw the chance to steal a march. They dismounted and went scrambling up the barricade and had barely reached the top when a rifle shot rang out beyond. It sent them driving back into cover, and Sperling swore.

"Dont' try it!" a voice shouted from the other side. It was Jeb Pelton's, Sperling realized. "We can knock you off as fast as you show yourselves!"

A wave of bitterness washed through Sperling as he realized he was stopped, at least at this pass. His riders came slithering back down to where he stood. He knew that money could not induce them to storm the barricade in hope of knocking out Pelton and whomever he had with him.

"What're we gonna do?" Godfrey said in a worried undertone. He obviously had had enough, and the others seemed to share his feeling.

"Go back to the herd for the time being," Sperling snapped.

The upset was wholly unacceptable, and Sperling fumed inwardly during the long ride down the mountain to where the herd was being held and guarded by Yerington's strong force. The foreman saw them coming and rode out to meet them. He had been waiting for word to bring on the cattle but was not surprised that it had not come.

"What did you run into?" he asked.

"They figure they've been pretty smart!" Sperling said with vehemence. "And maybe they outsmarted themselves! I'm going to give 'em so much worry about their own steers they won't have time to think about mine." It was something he would not have done a day ago, he knew, for he had a cowman's natural concern for cattle, no matter whose they were. But they had crowded him to it, the nesters, Penny—all of them.

"How you gonna work that?"

Sperling sat for a moment watching the herd that, unaware of the excitement swirling around it, had bedded for the night. "You'll move the critters down to the Gap. It'll look like we decided to go through the easiest opening. The plagued nesters'll have to gather there if they expect to stop us again. You'll leave enough men to move in fast. You'll take the rest and go across Dogleg. You'll start on that end of the mesa and shove every critter in your way on south. You'll keep shovin' till you've run it all so far into the desert, where there's no water, the stuff'll lack the strength to get back."

Yerington was staring in amazement. "But Hock, that'd take time. The nesters'd give us cain before we could get it finished."

"They'd have to leave the Gap open, and that'd be our chance to shove the herd in where we want it."

After a moment Yerington said in a moderated voice, "I reckon I see what you mean."

Chapter 11

JEB LAY in a rock nest against the north wall of the canyon, keenly watching the barricade he and the nesters had worked desperately to build against a second invasion of their range. They had spilled everything loose they could find into the canyon here at its narrowest point. Afterward Trace Getty had taken all but him and Matt Corey to the West Fork, since it was probable Sperling would attempt to seize and clear a pass before trying to send cattle through it.

Presently Matt called quietly from the other side of the stricture, "Think they pulled out?"

"Hard to tell."

For grim seconds they had waited to see whether the Dollarmark gunhands would pull back after the warning. Afterward Jeb had not been able to hear anything, and there was a dangerous chance that sharpshooters would lie hidden, waiting for someone to grow confident and show himself. On the other hand, if Dollarmark left he wanted to know where they went. He took off his hat and lifted it high enough to show and nothing happened. Presently he rose, his rifle ready, intently watching the top of the barricade. Only the night wind's tumbling in the timber above carried to him, and nothing moved at the barrier. Bent over, he ran across to where Matt was forted up.

"Guess it looked too tough for 'em," he said. "They're apt to try their luck at West Fork or the Gap, and I'd like to know just what."

"Get ridin'," Matt said. "They ain't likely to show here again, but if they do I can hold 'em off a spell."

"Be back as soon as I can."

Jeb left the rifle with Matt and hastened down the canyon, came to a break in the wall and climbed on top where their saddle horses waited. The motion felt good. The long, cramped wait since nightfall had worn on him, and the few moments of crucial tension had had their own effect. He sprang to the saddle and turned toward the summit, riding quietly as yet. Once he reached the west slope he reined in and sat listening intently. It was too windy for him to hear any indication of travel, but that would cover his own movement, too. He went on at a canter, bearing toward the holding ground of the steers ticketed for Muleshoe.

When at last he reached the rim, where once before he had done his spying, it was to see below in the pale moonlight a scene of great commotion. Riders were harrying the steers, raising them up from their sleep. North of them a large, huddled group of mounted men were in consultation. Presently most of these swung away and headed north along the foot of the Sapphires, over two dozen, he estimated. They meant to try one of the other mountain crossings and were moving the cattle into position to be ready for a quick follow-through if they seized one.

He dogged the forward party for two miles, while they rode steadily northward, convincing him that they were not returning to headquarters. Thereafter he cut a slant up the slope, making for the West Fork pass. This was higher than Thimble and, like the Gap, more of an open finger depressing the summit than a gorge like Thimble. Its open nature made its defense more difficult, and since it lay directly back of Buff Corey's place Corey had undertaken it, helped by Mark and Luke. Jeb approached the timber, entered it, and rode on swiftly until he could see the low saddle for which he was bound. As he neared it he halted and rode his horse in a short circle, the signal of identification the nesters had agreed upon. Then he headed into the pass.

Corey and his two wildling sons waited there, watching him intently. "Somethin' up, Jeb?" the father called forward.

Jeb rode on to them. "Dollarmark tried Thimble and decided it was too hot a proposition," he said. "Now they're bearin' this way, headed for here or the Gap, and the herd's trailin' 'em. One way or other, they mean to get it done tonight."

Corey let out a sigh. "The sooner it's settled the better. Matt all right?"

Jeb nodded. "We only had to fire a warnin' shot and they pulled out. If they've picked this pass next, we won't have it that easy. I'm goin' back to watch 'em. If they swing this way, I'll fire a shot to let you know and head back."

All the way down the slope Jeb expected to raise the Dollarmark night riders ahead of him at any moment. When he did not, he began to suspect that they were making for the Gap, the easiest passage for the herd and the hardest of all to defend. If he could be sure of that, he would go back and take a couple of the Coreys to the Gap with him.

As yet that was too long a guess, and he rode on. The

83

rim had played out where he came down to the edge of the basin, but the more open country let him see the horseback party he sought, on to the north and still traveling. They had made faster time than he had expected, and he saw that he would not be able to return to the pass behind and still warn the men guarding the Gap.

He decided to follow the night riders and, when they turned toward the Gap, to fire a couple of shots to confuse and worry them about their rear and also alert the nesters at the Gap. He set his pace to match theirs, watching constantly and seeing no sign that they had caught onto him. The trees marking the course of Sperling Creek soon loomed ahead. To his surprise the forward riders made no change toward the yawning gap from which the stream flowed. Presently they vanished into the trees, suggesting that they meant to use the cover to sneak in on the nesters in the Gap.

Jeb spurred his horse and sent it driving forward, coming into the timber upstream from where the Dollarmark men had entered it. Pulling down, he could hear nothing but the wind and the faint babble of the creek, so he emerged on the far side of the tree belt. He frowned, puzzled. The night riders were now moving on a tangent toward Dogleg Mountain, the prominence that with Sapphire abutted the main route to Muleshoe Mesa.

Understanding came to him with a shock. They meant to cross to the mesa over the trail the nesters used back and forth from the plateau. Either they were starting a diversionary attack on the nester cattle, or they meant to assault the Gap from the rear. Or it could be the West Fork pass, which the oncoming herd had not yet reached. Jeb's lips pinched grimly.

Bearing in mind the two men Sperling had posted on the west end of the Gap, after the nester cattle had been shoved through, he circled back across the creek and came in on the passage from the south, riding over the toe of the mountain and dropping into the pass. The shadows there concealed him, and he felt his nerves tighten as he rode on toward the nester-held end. But the sound of his horse threw itself forward, and presently a voice rang out in sharp challenge.

"Hold up!"

"It's Pelton, Swede," Jeb called back.

Two men rose from the footslopes on either hand, where they had been hidden in the rocks and brush, positioned and ready to lace the passage with a hot crossfire. They came down to him, and Swede Jorgan's companion proved to be Leet Teebo.

"Where's Getty?" Jeb asked.

"Him and Jimmy Hooker's back at the fire," Jorgan answered. "Why're you comin' in from that side?"

Jeb told them what had happened and what he expected and rode on. The guards here, standing watches in pairs, had built a fire against the night cold near the mesa end of the canyon. Getty and Hooker were there, drinking coffee. When they recognized him they sprang to their feet, Getty's unfriendliness showing plainly for a moment before he wiped it off.

"Thought it was Swede or Leet," Getty said. "What's up?"

"Most of Dollarmark's movin' this way," Jeb told him and went on to explain. "Sperling wants to spread us so thin we'll be helpless."

Getty's face took a bitter twist.

Dismally, Hooker said, "Looks like he's done it already. If we stick to the passes, they can run off our steers. If we try to stop that, they can bring the herd in. What're we gonna do?"

"Some guessing," Jeb said, "and hope we're right."

"What's yours?" Getty asked with a stare.

"Only that this is the pass they'll aim at, and that Jimmy's right about their tactics. If we try to break up the raid on our cattle, we've got to let theirs come through. If we hold the Gap, they'll run our stuff off, and this time into the desert. That's our choice."

"You got one?" Getty asked.

"Not that I like making. If we hold Sperling's cattle on his side of the mountain, we've got a show to bring ours back before bad weather. If we leave the passes to try to protect our stuff, he can move in and concentrate on moving our stuff off later."

Getty pondered a moment then, to Jeb's surprise, nodded his head. One thing about him was thoroughly convincing, Jeb reflected. He wanted to hit Hock Sperling where it would hurt the worst. Rubbing his jaw, Getty said, "Me and Jimmy'll go up there with Swede and Leet. There's time to get a couple of Coreys down here before the herd shows up. You want to go up after 'em?"

"Sure, Jeb agreed.

Getty and Hooker caught up their rifles and went swinging up the canyon on foot. Jeb took time for a cup of coffee. He rolled and lighted a cigarette, lost in thought, then swung back aboard his horse and headed south along Muleshoe, clinging to the foot of the mountain. From time to time he stopped to scan the country behind but could see or hear nothing in the obscurity to suggest Sperling's night riders. Presently the dark structures of Corey's headquarters loomed ahead in the moonlight, and he quartered toward the upper creek where it came out of the mountain. Soon he was following the trail beside the stream, climbing toward the pass.

He rode through the summit notch and came down on the other side to where Corey waited with his sons. He told them what he had seen and what Getty wanted and suggested that they wait where they were until they were sure the Dollarmark cattle passed this point and went on. They could still cross the mountain and reach the Gap before the plodding herd could get there.

"What you gonna do?" Corey asked.

"It's sure they've passed up Thimble Pass, at least for tonight, so I figured to pick up Matt."

From there he could ride the ridge to Thimble, where he found Matt cold and bored with standing guard on the barrier, and more than willing to trade it for something more exciting. "Big job roundin' up the mesa," he commented. "Gonna take 'em all night."

Jeb nodded. "I thought you and me might make something out of that, Matt, if you're as game as I think you are."

"Name your caper," Matt said promptly.

"If we could mix up Sperling's herd, the job of bustin' up the raiders would be a lot easier."

"Think we could?"

"We could try."

"Then let's get tryin'."

They had climbed on top of the canyon bluff to the waiting horses and were soon riding swiftly along the ridge toward the West Fork pass. By then the big Sperling herd had passed on north, and the other Coreys had left for the Gap. Jeb slanted thereafter, Matt riding silently beside him. When finally they caught sight of the plodding cattle they were less than two miles from the Gap. The Dollarmark riders would want to have the herd in place and ready to shove through before they set out to clear the passage to the mesa. The two nesters edged along through the thin timber at the foot of the mountain, pulling nearer, and Jeb explained what he had in mind.

They rode on out behind the herd, no longer hurrying but going fast enough to catch up with the drag before very long. It was a dangerous sally, but Jeb hoped the open approach would make the drag riders think they were somebody coming out from Dollarmark headquarters. The smell of dust grew heavy, and presently he saw a man riding along unconcernedly ahead of him. It had not occurred to the fellow to expect interference from the rear. Jeb hurried his horse and was nearly up on the man before he was discovered. The puncher wheeled his horse, but the first thing he saw was the gun in Jeb's lifted hand, dimly and grimly eloquent in the moonlight.

"Keep quiet," Jeb warned.

"What's going on here: *Pelton!*"

"Pull your gun and toss it away, then climb down from the horse."

He had made his impact on the Dollarmark crew on his first day in the basin, Jeb realized, for the man swung out of the leather in haste. Matt caught the reins of the horse, and at Jeb's clipped command the puncher started walking to the rear. Like most gunhands, he was plenty meek without the weapon that gave him bravado.

Matt let out a gusty sigh.

They were on the side of the herd toward the mountain, and the swing man on that side was well ahead. Observing that the riderless horse was a starface, Jeb changed to it since the Dollarmark hands would recognize it even before they identified the man in the saddle, and that would help in his next move.

"Hold back," he told Matt. "Then, if I have luck, come up."

He rode forward at once, with the floating dust thinner along the flank of the herd but still in evidence. Presently he saw ahead of him a rider trailing along beside the snailing column of steers. Off to the right the mountain was flattening out, showing that the Gap was not far ahead. But the point men were not slanting toward it, apparently meaning to halt the herd and hold it out of harm's way until the nesters were cleaned out of the pass or drawn out on the far side by the raiders on the mesa.

The Dollarmark man scarcely looked at him as he rode up, the starface fooling him, and again Jeb's gun was fisted. His voice snapped out.

"One wrong move, and you're dead."

"Jeb Pelton!" the puncher gasped. "What you doing on Rake's cayuse?"

"Never mind that."

The puncher had one wild moment of impulse then subsided and followed orders, ridding himself of his gun and quitting his horse. Matt hurried forward, then, and the two nesters were in virtual control of this side of the long column of cattle. Jeb hoped to break the line between the swing and point, and he rode forward, Matt with him. When he reached the spot he considered right, they began to crowd their horses in on the cattle. The animals edged over but continued to follow the line ahead. The nesters kept pressing them, and finally the line parted, the uneasy animals that had broken it tossing their heads in confusion as they veered to the left.

Somebody's voice cracked through the dust.

"What's happenin' back there?"

"It's now or never," Jeb called to Matt. "Hit 'em!"

Their guns blazing, they charged their horses directly at the fractured line. The jittery animals due ahead jumped and went driving away from them, heading west. Those behind began to snort as they caught the contagion. The running urge swept on to the rear, and the

88

whole rearward column exploded in a mass effort to escape the bedlam.

A moment later the shorter, forward column began to lose formation. Men's angry shouts punctuated the bellering, and there was shooting now from Dollarmark guns. But suddenly what had been a line moving north was a flying, senseless mass pelting west, with the pass receding in its rear.

"That's all the luck we'll have," Jeb called to Matt. "Head for the Gap."

There were at least four Dollarmark punchers still on horseback. Caught flatfooted, they had fought the panicked herd desperately, then bent their efforts to get disentangled from its trampling mass. Now they were waspishly free to consider the troublemakers. Jeb had that in mind and since he had tempted Matt into the reckless sortie, he preferred to run for it. Even as the two drove out, heading for the dark notch between the mountains, guns began to bark behind them.

A thing that worried him even more was the men Sperling had posted on this end of the canyon to guard against the nesters' trying to bring their own displaced cattle back through to Dogleg Plateau. To avoid them, he bent their course toward the mountain slope just south of the pass. The Dollarmark riders gave it up when their quarry faded into the timber. Jeb and Matt reined in to blow their horses, and Matt's excited laugh cracked the silence.

"Whatever's happened to our stuff," he said, "we've danged near made it a draw already."

"Going to take 'em a while to get that herd back together," Jeb agreed. "But daylight's not far off, which'll help 'em do it. That was good going, Matt. You'll do to ride the river with."

"Your idea," Matt said with a grunt. "All I done was come along for the ride."

Of all the nesters, Jeb reflected, the Coreys impressed him next after Cash Donovan. Jorgan, Teebo and Hooker were good men, with plenty of spunk and nerve, but they lacked the kind of fiery spirit he liked to see in a man and even in a woman. They were easily led, as Trace Getty had proved, and too blindly loyal and tractable. In the showdown that was bound to come between himself and Getty, he might have need of the Coreys, now that Cash was out of the picture.

They filed along the slope, made their identity known to the nesters gathered in the Gap and joined them. The others had heard shooting and the racket of running cattle but, from their position, had been unable to see what was happening. They were elated but knew, as Jeb did, that the climax here had only been postponed. Yet it had bought them a chance to protect their own cattle, for two men could hold the Gap until Dollarmark was ready to threaten it again.

Chapter 12

YEARS OF tenure had given Hock Sperling an intimate acquaintance with Muleshoe Mesa, and at the last moment he had decided to let Yerington handle the herd and take charge of this sally, himself. When he brought his riders off Dogleg Mountain at the source of Head Creek, he halted them for last minute instructions. There were nineteen of them, every man he had been able to scrape up after allowing Yerington a skeleton crew. It was to obtain such an outweighing advantage as this that he had carried twice his normal crew for the past months.

"Some of you know this side of the mountain," he said, "and some don't, so I'll explain it a little. Mesa Creek's the main stream and all the others over here empty into it and run south into the desert where it drains into a sink. The main stem's got a wide wash, and I want you to fan out on either side and throw everything into it. The banks are too high in most places for the nesters to break up our gather once it's in it, and I intend to have plenty of guards besides that. You understand?"

A general murmur told him they did.

"All right," the old man continued. "You'll miss some

90

stuff in the poor light, but that won't matter. We can weed it out later. Now rattle your hocks. I want you to have everything in the wash and way south by daylight."

He watched them divide in two groups, one of which crossed the creek to work the other side from there to the south end of the mesa. He waited until the last of them vanished into the bad light before he let his shoulders slump under their load of fatigue.

There was scarcely a chance that Dollarmark could have made so many movements without the nesters catching onto what was stirring. It made little difference, he mused, whether they chose to keep the herd out of the pass or to attack this movement or both. He could handle them. If he was held up one place he could proceed in another. It would all come out to the same place: Dollarmark restored to what it had been before grasping little men nearly brought it to ruin.

Nonetheless he did not want to be taken by surprise if he could avoid it, and presently he pulled his shoulders stiff and straight again and rode south to Rooster Knob, from which he could see the mesa end of the Gap even in this light. There he dismounted and settled himself with his back against a juniper tree. He fished out a cigar and clamped it in his teeth but left it unlighted.

He had been there half an hour when he saw a horseman come out of the Gap and turn south along the footslope. Alert instantly, Sperling climbed to his feet, staring out through the faulty illumination. There was a nester and, while Dollarmark's riders had not yet worked down this far, he could make trouble. Sperling tightened the cinch of his saddle, stepped across the horse and rode off the knob, slipping behind the brush of a shallow wash. This let him angle toward the rider, who pressed steadily southward, and by hurrying he came abreast of him. Once the man stopped to take a long look to the rear, and Sperling got the strong impression that he was Jeb Pelton.

The old man's mouth pinched bitterly. Pelton had bought into the quarrel because he blamed Dollarmark for the killing of his brother, but he had no part in the range dispute whatsoever. Yet he was the best man on the nester side, which made his wrongmindedness all the more intolerable. Sperling dogged him until, near Corey's place, Pelton—if it was he—turned right into the creek canyon. Whatever he was up to, he was not pitting himself against the night roundup, at least not yet.

It dawned on him that Pelton was getting men from the other passes, either to concentrate them at the Gap or for some other purpose. That decided Sperling to learn a little more about this business, and he put his horse toward the same canyon Pelton had entered. As he climbed the cold seemed to penetrate him more deeply, and he wondered if it was the elevation or a marked drop in temperature or just his accursed age. He watched the climbing canyon ahead of him closely, listening with care, but reached the summit before he heard horses coming his way.

Luckily he was where he could pull off the trail easily, and he slipped into the adjoining pines, dismounting and standing so he could keep his horse quiet. Three riders appeared, passing close enough to let him recognize Buff Corey and two of his sons. Sperling stood frowning, wondering what had become of Pelton, who was the man to watch. He waited until the Coreys had dropped into the east canyon, strongly suspicious that Pelton had descended on the basin side. The thought bothered him. Instead of going into alarmed, head-on action, the nesters seemed to be moving quietly and with purpose. Did they have the nerve to strike at him where he was the most vulnerable, in that moving herd or against Dollarmark headquarters which Trace Getty had once threatened to burn? Suddenly less confident of the night's outcome, Sperling decided to drop down on the basin side.

He emerged on the bottom just as the herd moved into view and rode out and joined Lot Yerington, who was on the right point. The foreman was surprised to see him, but Sperling made a reassuring motion with his hand.

"The boys're at work on the mesa," he said, falling in beside Yerington, "and no trouble so far. But the nesters are congregating for something, and Pelton's rattling around loose, and that man worries me."

"Don't know what he can do," Yerington said gruffly. "There ain't enough of 'em to pull anything that'd hurt much."

"Right now," the old man said dryly, "we're stretched a little thin, too. Seems to me it's a lot colder all at once. You notice it?"

Yerington nodded. "Might get a freeze-up. Sure hope it holds off till we've got this shook down."

The old worry about the new steers he had to winter safely, the loss of which would throw him into deep financial trouble again, rose in Sperling's uneasy mind. Usually he had a steel grip on his nerves, and now their jumpiness angered him. The plodding herd was coming along serenely, guarded by half a dozen tough men. Everything off toward headquarters looked all right, and the drivers were only a mile from the Gap.

His first awareness that there was basis for his uneasiness came when, down the column behind, a man's voice ripped out, "What's happenin' back there?" and at once the explosion of guns rent the night.

Sperling swung his horse, stunned and bewildered. Not far down the column two riders were driving their horses insanely into the moving string of cattle and emptying their pistols into the air. *Traitors!* he thought furiously and reached for his own gun, but at that moment the whole herd down that way came apart. Yerington had sent his horse driving along the flank of the yawing cattle closer at hand, and Sperling bent his own efforts to keep the point steers in order. Dust boiled over him, and the thudding run of hoofs told him there was no hope of holding them, either.

He whipped his horse about again, determined to deal with the betrayers the nesters had somehow planted on him. By then he saw the two men driving toward the Gap and he sent shot after shot toward them. Other and loyal riders emerged from the dust, having disentangled themselves from the run, and they also shot at the fugitives. Yerington rode up to him, and Sperling swore bitterly.

"I'll get those turn-coat sons and hang them!" he vowed.

93

Yerington shook his head. "None of our boys done that."

They both saw the two dismounted men running toward them across the prairie to the south. Sperling and his foreman rode to meet them, and presently the old man knew what had become of Jeb Pelton.

In the first pale daylight Jeb sat his horse on Rooster Knob, keenly scanning the sweep of the mesa now illuminated. Six of the nesters were with him, Jorgan and Teebo having been left at the Gap to hold it until Dollarmark was in position to try to breach it again. Trace Getty sat restless in his saddle next to Jeb. He had been wildly impatient for action after the success in breaking up the Dollarmark herd, but Jeb had pointed out that it would be no such quick job for the Sperling outfit to clean the nester cattle off the mesa. Since daylight had been close at hand it had seemed sensible to wait until they could see what they had to deal with, and his advice had prevailed.

Now they could not see a steer or horse anywhere in the country visible from their high viewpoint.

"They sure worked fast," Corey said.

"They had a lot of men," Jeb said, but that did not satisfy him completely. A thought occurred to him, and he mused a moment before adding, "The main creek runs down a pretty big wash, as I remember it."

"That's right," Getty agreed. "Mesa Creek. It's wash is wide and deep."

"What they might have done," Jeb resumed, "was fan down the edges of the mesa and swept everything into the wash in the center. That wouldn't take so long. It'd make the gather easier to control and to keep us away from. They've got that far along, at least on this end, but it's not likely they're off Muleshoe yet."

"Sperling's a crafty old fox," Corey said. "That sounds like his doing. They'll have so many guns on either side of the wash we can't come close to the critters."

"We can plug the wash ahead of 'em!" Getty said.

"Sure," Jeb agreed. "Until they drive us out. They've got men enough to do it and kill half of us in the bargain."

"We ain't gonna set on our tails and let them run our

94

steers off!" Hooker complained, and the others appeared to agree with him.

Jeb shared their feelings but had a nagging suspicion that this time the balance was going to tip Sperling's way. "Let's see if we've figured it right, first," he temporized. "And we'd best keep out of sight."

They filed off the knob and rode over into the foot timber of Sapphire, which now was brightening in the bitter cold morning. The lack of food and rest told on them, and they were silent and grumpy. They passed thus behind Corey's place, still seeing no cattle nor sign of riders along the wash, which lay over in the eastern distance. Then, half an hour later, they saw a heavy dust hanging over the plain, about a mile on south of them.

"You pegged it right," Jeb," Corey said. "Them cutbanks are high and steep from there on, and the steers couldn't get out if they tried."

"The only thing we can do," Getty said, "is keep out of sight till the wash fans out at the sink. They might turn 'em loose there, anyhow. What do you say, Jeb?"

"You boys know this end of the country, and I don't. But I do know we can't take them steers away from Dollarmark right now. If they turn 'em loose at the sink, we can pick 'em up and head back. If they still hold onto 'em, we've got a better chance to make a fight."

They rode on along the mountain.

The country south of that point changed rapidly. Sapphire Mountain grew nude of timber and moved farther west, and the plain running eastward turned into a flat monotony, sterile except for runty desert growth that supported only rodent and reptilian life. This piece of wasteland ran for forty miles before good rangeland began again, a blast furnace in summer and in winter a race course for killing winds.

Jeb had heard about it but not until he had ridden on with the nesters for another hour, drawing well ahead of the herd, did he get the full, forbidding impact. The Coreys were the most familiar with it, and they led the way, keeping close to the mountain until the cover gave out, then striking boldly across the desert toward the sink. This proved to be a vast marshland of putrid water joining a flat dry lake bed white with minerals deposited

95

by centuries of evaporation. Only in flood seasons did it receive water, Corey said. It was mean country to let cattle move into too far or for a man to be set down in afoot.

A cuesta formation ranked along the west edge of the marsh, giving the nesters elevation and a place to conceal themselves and their mounts. From there Jeb could see the wash and the dust cloud hanging over it, maybe two miles to the north.

"From the speed they're makin'," Corey said anxiously, "the critters must be plenty tired. Sperling don't aim to leave enough strength in 'em for 'em to make it back."

Jeb was worried about that prospect, himself. If they could get custody of the cattle soon enough, they could drift them back to water and grass before they played out completely. He hoped Dollarmark would be satisfied to drop them off here, for they were off Muleshoe and could be kept off once Sperling took possession and his many punchers were free to patrol its borders.

"I thought Sperling was a cattleman," he said roughly. "He might treat a nester like that, but I wouldn't think he would a steer."

"That old man's slipped," Corey said regretfully. "Brooded so much over the way he thinks he's been abused he don't see straight."

It seemed a long while before the lead cattle appeared where the big wash lost itself on the sandy margin of the marsh. The point riders held their positions and they and the first steers were all that could be seen because of the fat sausage of dust rolling up from the loose underfooting.

"They ain't gonna turn 'em loose, boys," Corey said with a groan.

"And this is the best chance we'll have to take over," Jeb added. "While the rest of the outfit's back in the dust."

"Yeah," Getty said tensely. "If we hit it now, we might pull back that herd. Come on!"

They shoved to their feet in full agreement, ran down the slope to their hidden horses, and sprang into the saddles. It was a desperation move, but the dust from the loose, drifting sand of this vicinity would help them, plus the fact that the Sperling riders might not expect trouble from the nesters at this late stage. Jeb knew what Getty meant by bulling back. Driven cattle, if confronted by something frightening due ahead, would often swap ends and take off in the opposite direction, what had been the point of the drive becoming the drag of a stampede.

The nesters went down the grade like screeching Indians, curving in on the herd's line of march then charging head on. Jeb saw the horse of a point rider rear on its hind legs, and the lead steers skidded to a stop. In the space of a breath the cattle in front were leaping on those behind, trying to get back into the dust. The point riders began shooting, but the nesters drove on. Momentarily the herd was at a standstill, and dust boiled forward to cover all of it, and the nesters charged recklessly into the pall.

Guns crackled to the rear, and Jeb let out a groan. Recovered from the first surprise, the Sperling hands were bent on stampeding the cattle sidewise, instead of letting them be turned back toward the mesa. The country eastward was only a little less forbidding than the deathtrap south of the sink.

He was thundering straight up the right flank of the roiling cattle, hungrily hunting a target for his gun, and this was the direction Dollarmark was trying to turn the creatures. There were Sperling men on this side, too, but they were not shooting and concentrated on getting out of the way. He swung around and found that the other nesters had followed him.

"Back!" he shouted against the uproar. "They were too quick for us, this time!"

It was the counsel of wisdom, for they were barely in the clear when the herd found alignment and went thundering by.

Nothing more could be done about them while the landscape swarmed with Sperling riders. Jeb counted noses and saw that all of his comrades were there, trying to clear their throats and lungs of the dust.

"Somebody sure thought fast," Hooker said in a rusty voice.

Corey shook his head. "Old Hock again. He must

have figured on us being smart enough to wait till they got out of the wash to tackle 'em, and given orders to run the stuff due east. Which is nearly as bad as where they'd of wound up otherwise. Boys, if *we're* smart we'll skeedaddle before they get around to tackling us."

Again there was agreement, and the badly outnumbered nesters went driving toward the distant slope of Sapphire Mountain.

Chapter 13

THEY WERE exhausted men and fully realized it when they reached Buff Corey's place on the West Fork. The dismal morning was half gone, and a chilling wind had risen to stream bitterly along the mesa, which meant that the temperature on the unsheltered basin side was lower yet. Corey and his sons built a fire and set about fixing a meal, and Jimmy Hooker began to doze in his chair.

Tired as he was, there was a notable restlessness in Trace Getty. "Well, we got to hand it to you, Jeb," he said with surprising generosity, "for giving old Sperling as much to worry about as he gave us. Come morning, this country's apt to be froze solid. With this wind Sperling's gonna put every tough hand he's got to gathering steers for a new try. That at least gets their hot breath off our necks a while."

"Our stuff ain't gonna be so cozy," Corey said tartly. "If this wind keeps up, the steers'll start driftin' south. Into the very country we kept it out of this morning."

"We've got as good a show to bring it back to the mesa," Getty said, untroubled, "as he's got to bring his blasted critters over."

Again Jeb had the uneasy feeling that the man was more eager to hurt Sperling than he was to help his nester neighbors. He never grew as excited as he was when he saw danger to the big cattleman and a chance to exploit it and hurt him. More than once Jeb had had the impression that Getty's real interest in the nesters

98

lay in the fact that they backed him and, at least until his own arrival, had relied entirely on the mysterious man's leadership. Buck Gillidge's remark about the Judas steer that led its own kind to slaughter had become cemented in Jeb's mind. Although he could not put his finger on the precise cause as yet, the label did not seem farfetched.

They ate their breakfast, with quantities of hot coffee, which somewhat restored them. Afterward it was decided that Jeb and Getty would go up to relieve Jorgan and Teebo at the Gap. The others would sleep a while, then come up to relieve them for their turn. There had been a chance that Sperling would leave men to see that the nester cattle were not rounded up and brought back, but the threateningly frigid wind would offset that. He would need every hand he could scrape up to gather his own cattle and get them into the sheltered area east of Sapphire that he coveted. Jeb hoped an opportunity would develop from that fact.

He and Getty were nearly to the eastern end of the Gap when Getty rose suddenly on the stirrups, staring off to the north with a frown.

"Smoke comin' out of my chimney," he muttered. "Wonder what that means."

"We better see," Jeb said.

Getty nodded, and they went on past the Gap, riding at a fast lope for the little ranch headquarters on the bank of Head Creek. A horse stood in front of Getty's shack, and when he saw it Getty grunted and slowed down.

"It's all right. That's Anita's cayuse."

Cold spread through Jeb's shoulders. "I wonder if it went the wrong way for Cash."

Getty said nothing, and they rode on up to the little shack. Anita opened the door and looked out, then came onto the stoop. Jeb saw that she carried a gun in a hip holster. Her expression held nothing disturbing.

"Hello," she said, only glancing at Jeb and fixing her attention on her half-brother.

"Somethin' wrong?" Getty asked.

"Not wrong. I thought you would like to know Cash is past the crisis. Doc says he'll make it, now."

"Thank the Lord," Jeb breathed. "Can he move yet?"

"No. But he won't be crippled, either."

Jeb felt like a thousand pounds had been lifted from his shoulders. Cash would be on the shelf a long time, recuperating. But, if he was to come back to the little spread they now owned jointly, this fight would mean a lot more personally than the finding of Tom Pelton's murderer.

"I made myself some coffee," Anita was saying, "and you fellows look cold."

"I reckon we can take a few minutes, Jeb," Getty said, swinging down. "The boys at the Gap had it softer than we did. This is bad country for you to travel alone, Sis."

"I came out the nester road," she replied as they went indoors, Jeb following. "Your house is a mess, Trace. Don't you ever clean it?"

"Been pretty busy lately."

"What's the latest?"

They stood by the fire with steaming coffee in their hands while Getty explained the struggle for possession of Muleshoe Mesa, Sperling's last objective and the nesters' last stand. She listened somberly.

"Cash has been fretting about it," she said. "Penny's awfully worried, too."

"She still sore at the old man?"

"That's too weak a word. She's heartbroken. That proud, stubborn old devil! Right's what he says it is, and he doesn't mind who he hurts enforcing it. What gives some men such faith in their own convictions?"

Jeb sipped his coffee. He had been aware that she was ignoring him pointedly while she centered her attention on Getty. Now he was keenly conscious of the double meaning in her question. His suspicions of Getty still stuck in her craw, and she was continuing to make it plain what she thought of them and him.

"You've got to say one thing for strong convictions," he murmured. "They make strong men."

"Or pigheaded ones, with no consideration for anyone but themselves." She realized she had reached him, and there was a faint pleasure in her eyes.

"That could be. How're the pots?"

"I haven't done much lately."

"I still wonder how many dollars' worth I busted for you the night I blundered around in your shop."

"Don't let it worry you."

She was permitting no basis for friendliness, and he shrugged.

They saw her as far as Dogleg Mountain, on her return ride to Broken Rock, then went on to relieve the guard at the Gap. Shortly after noon Buff and Matt Corey showed up to take over, and Jeb went to Getty's place with him to sleep for a couple of hours. He was too tired to let go immediately and lay on a bunk in the warm shack listening to the ever-strengthening wind.

It seemed early for snow to fly, but he knew that this region lay in a wind belt that often brought down bad weather. The cold, while a grim reminder of worse to come, might not turn killing yet. But the wind would drift the nester cattle into a death trap that was bound to be effective: the desert around and south of the sink. Something had to be done speedily about that.

His delayed sleeping caused him to waken to find Getty up ahead of him and busy at the stove. The smell of coffee and frying bacon blended with the smoky heat of the room. When Jeb sat up Getty turned around, an easy amiability on his face.

"Have us a bait of grub in a minute," he said.

"Been outside?"

"Yeah. The water bucket's froze tight, and it lacks a couple of hours till dark."

"That means the waterholes will be frozen before morning."

"Likely. We got to try and fetch our stuff back. If we can't cut it right off, we'll have to leave herders to bust ice and keep 'em from driftin'. Buff and his boys and Jimmy Hooker are the ones for that. They know the country."

Getty had made sourdough biscuits, and he put them on the table with a plate of bacon and the coffee pot. They ate silently in the way of rangemen and when they were finished, Getty eyed Jeb thoughtfully.

"You and Sis could hit it off," he commented.

Jeb glanced at him sharply, wondering why that had

101

been introduced. When he said nothing, Getty shook his head.

"She's a great gal. I never understood why she likes to play with mud all the time, but she does. That's all it takes, I guess."

"She likes to make things with her hands," Jeb said. "She's good at it, and it gives her satisfaction. I can see that."

"You're a lot alike. More'n me and her, although we get along fine for only a half-way brother and sister. I hope you get to know her better."

Jeb's eyes narrowed as he wondered if Getty was holding Anita up as bait for him. *Lay off me, and my pretty sister will like you.* The thought angered him, and he said, "She trusts you and resents the fact that I don't. That don't influence what I think or what I'll do."

"You still think that I'm only grinding my own axe." The amiability was entirely gone.

"I made my sentiments plain the night you tried to run Dollarmark off the plateau and it blew up in your face. Nothing's happened to change them. But we see alike on one thing. We've got to stand up under Sperling's attacks and beat him. We've worked together all right on that, and we've got to keep on. Getting busy again right now."

Getty's eyes kindled with something he did not express otherwise. "Got a suggestion?"

Jeb nodded. "The others seem to need leaders. So let's divide the responsibility. You, the Coreys and Hooker try to save the steers. I know the basin and the passes Sperling can use. So let me, Jorgan and Teebo handle that end. We'll be enough till Dollarmark's got its cattle unscrambled and is ready to hit us again."

Getty considered a moment, then nodded. "Sounds sensible. We might get the steers back pretty fast, again we might not. If we can't, we got to find temporary shelter, water and graze out there. But you'd be pretty shorthanded here."

"Range is no good to us without cattle on it. If we lose one, we might as well lose both."

"That's right, I reckon. Let's get it organized."

Getty no longer seemed to resent the fact that Jeb was

102

still open in his distrust and dislike, but Jeb was positive it did not result from a lack of pride. Whatever the man had up his sleeve, it depended on beating Sperling first. He was willing to swallow resentments a while to make use of any help he could get to that end. Once he had Sperling where he wanted him, if that ever happened, it would be another story.

They found the others congregated at the Gap where they had been busy, Jeb saw. A shelter had been built of brush and canvas where they had their fire, and wind-breaks had been erected at the sentry posts deeper in the canyon. The Corey boys had prowled Sperling's end of the Gap to find that he had removed his gunguards from there, indicating his desperate need for men. Moreover, the large party that had swept the cattle off the mesa had returned to the basin, Corey said, going over the West Fork pass.

"That's the go-ahead signal for us," Getty said with satisfaction. "I hope our stuff ain't drifted bad."

"We better figure it has," Corey said.

All but Jeb, Jorgan and Teebo pulled out, strength-ened by the fact that they again had a fighting chance, however great the odds were against their success. Jeb hunkered at the fire, afterward, soaking up heat and thoughtfully smoking a cigarette. He was strongly curious about what was going on in the basin at the moment, and presently he rose and tossed the stub of the cigarette into the coals.

Riding up to where Jorgan and Teebo were posted, he said, "There's not apt to be trouble here tonight, and I'm checkin' out a while."

"Taking a look-see?" Jorgan said.

Jeb nodded. "They've had all day to work and must have got a herd started building. I'd like to know where they're holding it. Don't shoot me if I come back this way pretty fast."

"Just give the sign."

The sentry posts had been moved forward, now that Sperling had taken his men away from the basin end, and were situated where their occupants had a good view of the western approaches. Jeb rode out of the draw, presently passing the deserted tent Dollarmark had put up for its own guards. He moved on down Sperling Creek, and as he came into the open the immediately deepened cold of the wind hit him with numbing force. The day was fading rapidly from the wan grey sky. The creek slipped along beside him, and he kept to its brushy cover, reaching the point where he and Matt had scattered the Dollarmark steers and going on.

He rode with hunched shoulders, his thoughts drifting back to the days when Hock Sperling had had the whole country to use to his best advantage. Viewed as a unit— the basin, mesa, and separating mountains—it provided everything needed for a large cattle operation. Grass was everywhere, and water was no great problem. But weather had always been a different matter, as Sperling had learned painfully in the blizzard winters that came so close to ruining him.

Vast exposed sections in his end of the basin and his railroad land below Dogleg Plateau could not be used during deep winter. To stock them to capacity during amenable seasons, he needed a sufficient sheltered area to carry the same animals without loss of weight through the worst of the year. Some of this he still possessed in the south basin, and the rest had once been available in the creek breaks on Dogleg Plateau and the larger, mountain-sheltered Muleshoe Mesa.

Reduced as he had been the past several years, he had not felt the pinch. He could have gone on indefinitely operating a middle-sized cattle ranch, but he had not been satisfied with that. Now the excess cattle he had acquired had to be carried in the exposed sections, unless he regained the mesa or perilously overgrazed the limited sheltered areas he already had at hand.

Trace Getty had based his tactics on the fact that, to re-establish his old rights to Dogleg and Muleshoe, Sperling needed the cattle to stock the extra range immediately and that, to acquire the necessary steers, he had borrowed heavily. A big winter kill would certainly hurt him badly, an outcome the proud old tyrant would go to any end to avoid.

Considering this, Jeb began to see light. If Sperling could be cornered and made to realize that he had been, there lay a great opportunity for a Judas steer—a traitor. Hock Sperling would pay a stiff price, even if he had to borrow at the bank again, for an act of betrayal that would give him the mesa and save him at the last moment. Was Getty capable of it? In view of the record and his own instinct about it, Jeb was certain that the man was.

The light was fading, and Jeb was west of the road that ran north across Dogleg Plateau when, to his surprise, he saw a party of several horsemen riding south from the direction of Battle Creek, apparently aiming for Dollarmark headquarters. Puzzled as to why so many of them were over here when all hands were supposed to be unscrambling cattle in the main basin, he pulled down in the creek timber and sat thoughtfully until they had forded the creek above him and gone on. Then he changed directions, turning to the right and heading toward what had been and still was range that belonged to Cash and himself.

He came down into the Battle Creek valley well below the little shack Cash and Tom had built near its head, and at once he grew more mystified. This was range Sperling had stocked with the first herd he moved onto nester holdings, and in the weakening light there was not a steer in sight. He crossed the creek and turned up the valley on its far side and confirmed the fact that, for some reason, Dollarmark had emptied it.

On a hunch, he crossed the breaks to the next valley, which was that of Sagehen Creek, and there he came upon men pushing a growing gather of cattle up the creek toward Dogleg Mountain. Jeb pulled back hastily into the cover of a rock crop and stared hard into the growing dusk, his gaze fixed on the vague, forested land rise to the east. Dogleg was a lesser mountain than Sapphire, more rounded, but too high and exposed to be used for winter range. Yet this drive was headed for it, either to cross or to move south along its base toward the Gap. He let the cattle pass and fade into the dusk, then went on to the last creek valley. Again he came upon a cattle gather that was slowly moving up the valley toward Dogleg Mountain.

Undoubtedly Sperling was making this the herd he meant to cross next, although it seemed strange that he would collect it here from range he had just stocked for the winter, with considerable trouble, instead of from the badly overstocked basin on the south. It would not give him a herd any quicker and would render it necessary to make yet another roundup in the basin and move and distribute the gather here.

An explanation cracked in Jeb's mind like a lightning flash. If Sperling slipped a new herd onto Dogleg Mountain quietly, a move the nesters had not anticipated because of the bitter cold up there and its out-of-the-way location, the wind would drift the cattle south to come down on the mesa automatically. That would free his men to concentrate on keeping the nesters from interfering. The driving wind had shown the old man how to flank the hotly disputed passes, perhaps to accomplish this before it was even suspected. Once he held the vital mesa, he could reorganize the cattle left on this side at his leisure.

Chapter 14

JEB SAW in a flash that there was nothing he could do to break it up. Apparently the first batch of cattle had already gone onto the mountain from Battle Creek, and there were two more heavily manned drives on the move. They had only to take the steers onto the level top of Dogleg and turn them loose.

The creatures would try instinctively to get down out of the galling wind. They would turn with the blast and move with it instead of crossing it in an effort to get back down on this plateau. Even if the nesters could get together in time to fight them back, the oversized Dollar-mark crew would have its hands free to defeat them roundly. In his desperation, Hock Sperling had come up with a devastating slash.

These convictions firmed swiftly in Jeb's mind, but he knew they were based on guesswork. A way to verify or disprove them was to go back by way of the mountain and see if that first party had really turned steers loose up there. He returned to Battle Creek in what had now become full night. Reaching the stream, he turned and followed to its head. The dark had grown too deep for him to see fresh cattle sign as he climbed the slope, out of the creek canyon now and moving across the pine-dappled, slow rise of the mountain.

The basin had been colder than the mesa, and up here it was colder still, the wind that boiled in from the north grinding savagely in the timber. He was thoroughly chilled by the time he reached the crest and could put the killing blast to his back. He rode briskly and soon came on stolidly drifting cattle and knew he had figured it right.

There were a great many of them sifting through the timber close enough to see as he hurried past. Trying to turn so many back in the darkness would be like beating out a forest fire with a hat, and there was twice this number on the way. Presently he struck the trail by which the nesters regularly descended and soon dropped down into the warmer confines of the mesa.

After what he had experienced, riding into the Gap was like entering an enclosed room, with the wind shut out and the temperature notably higher. The fire at the shelter had nearly burned out, and he freshened it. Then he hurried on through the passage to where Jorgan and Teebo were keeping their cold watch. He told them quickly what he had stumbled onto.

"Sperling's made this position useless to us," he concluded, "by going around it. So there's no use wasting time here. Come back and warm yourselves while we figure out our best move."

"Well, there always was too few of us," Teebo said dismally, "and too blasted many of them."

They said no more until they were back at the fire and trying to thaw themselves in its heat, helping that along with strong black coffee from the pot that simmered on a rock by the coals.

"Would one of you be able to find Getty and his men?" Jeb asked the nesters.

They shook their heads, and Jorgan said, "Not at night. I've only got a foggy notion of the country over east, and I reckon that goes for Leet. It's up to us to do what we can, and it don't strike me that it'll be much."

"No use gettin' ourselves killed," Teebo added, "when we don't have a show, anyhow."

Jeb had the same opinion and did not try to raise their spirits with false cheer. He nodded. "We won't lose our heads, boys. But a man gets breaks he don't count on. Don't forget that."

Teebo shoved to his feet, muttering, "Take one big enough to run a train through to save us now."

"Won't find it by hidin', I guess," Jorgan said moodily. "Let's get on the mesa and see what happens."

They walked down to where the nesters' horses had been left in a natural shelter and presently rode back through the draw to the mesa. They had barely broken into the open when they reined in abruptly.

"There's your break!" Teebo said in a furious blast.

A red glow burned through the blackness in the direction of Buff Corey's place, too large to be anything but burning buildings. Jeb remembered the southbound party of riders who had first drawn his attention to the Dogleg plateau. Their work with the steers finished ahead of the other parties, that one had dipped south and gone over the West Fork pass.

"Why'd they have to do that?" Jorgan said, aghast.

"They'll go after Hooker's and Getty's, too!" Jeb said in driving voice. "They don't aim to leave us a headquarters —no shelter, no blankets, no grub! It's too late to do anything about Corey's, but the other places still look all right. Come on!"

There was no uncertainty in them now, for if they were robbed of the means to maintain themselves in the vicinity they certainly could do nothing about their range and steers. By common agreement they went driving across the open mesa toward Jimmy Hooker's headquarters on the east fork of Mesa Creek, which, closer to Corey's than was Getty's place, would be the arsonists' next objective. Nothing showed in that direction yet, but the Sperling hoodlums had a head start.

The steep banks of Mesa Wash held them up until they found a place to cross. From there the country lay flat and open except for a few lonely clumps of trees. They drove their horses mercilessly, fighting against a blow so staggering they could not hope to continue the fight if they did not somehow reduce its effects. Yet when they were still a mile away from Hooker's little ranch headquarters, a sudden daub of red appeared over there, and they knew they were too late.

"Trace Getty's place!" Jeb panted. "We can get there first and hold 'em off!"

They swung their horses hard to the left, knowing their last chance was their best one. Dogleg Mountain's southern end loomed far ahead of them, and the change headed them into a wind that was cold even here where the Mountain served to protect them. The first Dollarmark steers were coming down from the mountain when they reached Head Creek and turned upstream toward Getty's place. Jorgan let out a whoop when presently they saw that the buildings were still unmolested.

"Here's where we make our stand," Jeb said grimly as they reined in. "If we lose this place we've got nothing left at all." He ran his gaze over the structures they had to protect. Getty had not invested much here, putting up besides the shack a small barn with a couple of corrals attached to it. "I'll take the barn, you boys the house. Make up a bundle of grub and whatever ammunition he's got, in case we run out."

"What we gonna do with our cayuses?" Teebo asked.

"Barn. Those Dollarmark sons'll surround us, and we don't want the critters run off."

They dismounted and led the horses into the musty interior of the barn and stalled them. Jeb remained there while the others went over to the house, about two hundred feet to the east. He knew that the torch wielders would not be far behind them, for they would have headed this way immediately once Hooker's buildings were burning strongly. The wind would make it impossible to hear them come in, but from his position just inside the barn door he had a clear view of the mesa as far as the eye would reach in the bad light. There would be a moment's warning.

He stood pondering on Hock Sperling and the deterioration in the man's character since this bloody trouble broke out. In the move against Dogleg Plateau the man had still been sufficiently temperate to avoid unnecessary violence and destruction. Now nothing seemed past him, and he lacked even a prudent concern for the public opinion his ruthlessness here on the mesa would outrage. That was the flaw in a prideful man. In the end nothing mattered with him but to dominate, to rule and possess.

The oncoming horsemen soon took shape out in the vague, dark distance. There were half a dozen, about the number he had seen leaving the plateau and heading south. They were not men roused to desperation by looming defeat. These fellows liked things the way they were being done, would not mind if they got bloodier and dirtier yet.

They were not expecting trouble here and rode boldly in on the place. Preferring to let them come close enough for him to see when they scattered for cover, Jeb held fire until they were scarcely a hundred yards from him. Then he sent a shot whipping over their heads, the last warning he would give them. The guns of Jorgan and Teebo added threatening echoes, the blasts crashing through the whine of the wind in the timber above them.

The effect was that of a bomb burst over the carelessly crowded riders, and the reaction of the horses was as pronounced. They had come up where there was no immediate cover, and the animals reared and wheeled while the men on their backs tried to control them, to get their bearings and find protection. The nesters were not out for blood, even yet, and only peppered the ground and air about the Sperling men, who bolted in ignominious retreat to get out of range. But the raiders wheeled up at once, out there, dismounted and left their horses, informed that if they set yet another fire they would pay a stiff price first.

Jeb still stood in the barn's open doorway, back a little in the darkness, and neither he nor his comrades dared to waste ammunition. He watched the Sperling men separate in two groups and move off in either direction. Those on the east made for the brush along Head Creek, and the others moved so as to bring the barn between them and the shack. These last were his to handle, and they had decided on the move because there was no side opening in the barn.

The blank wall complicated matters for him also. When they had vanished, he slipped outside and slid along the front wall to the corner. Thereafter he stood in the cold wind, watching around the corner and waiting for somebody to fire at the structure or try to slip in to the wall in hope of setting a fire there that would probably spread to and wipe out the house.

Gunfire erupted beyond the house and was returned hotly. The diversion encouraged somebody in the brush off from the barn to fire a test shot into the side wall, to which Jet did not respond. There seemed a fair chance that they supposed the nesters all to be in the shack, and he waited patiently. In a moment he saw movement in the brush, then a man's dim figure materialized slowly.

The fellow turned his head for a moment as if speaking to somebody behind him, then began to come forward very carefully. Jeb let him emerge fully into view then set a shot scorchingly close to him, and the man made a precipitate dive into cover. That probably had dampened any enthusiasm for moving in from this side, but Jeb waited there, carefully watching around the corner of the building.

A man yelled from the brush, "Pour it into the sons! They got this side covered, too! We'll have to gun 'em out!"

Even as the call died away on the wind, Jeb laced the brush with gunfire, then stepped back into concealment while he worked shells out of his gunbelt and reloaded. All six of the Dollarmark hands were whacking lead into the buildings now. Since they insisted on having it that way, he reflected, the time had come to shoot to hit the mark.

He slipped to the back end of the barn, speaking quietly to the nervous horses, and reached a door used for removing manure. The heaped cleanings all but blocked the view to the rear, but they also hid him when he slipped out and moved in between the pile and the barn corner. The men on the other side were peppering

111

the shack, and Jeb stood motionless for a breath, keening his immediate surroundings.

A blob of fire punctured the darkness at the brush, out from him, and he shot at it instantly. A man's involuntary outcry echoed the explosion, then two guns at that spot were throwing lead his way. He shot again and ducked back, immediately moving behind the manure pile while they wasted ammunition on the spot where he had stood. Again he fired and abruptly the men in the brush gave it up. Immediately afterward the firing at the shack died away, as well.

The Sperling gunhands had become convinced that this would be no easy thing, and time was on their side. Other Dollarmark men would move down here as they got through with the cattle, and some of them could show up at any moment. He went back to the front of the barn and from there saw two men moving across his field of vision, to the south but out of range, down where they had left their horses. They supported another man who limped along between them, apparently hit in the leg. They helped him mount, and the wounded man rode off toward the nearby slope of Dogleg Mountain. He was going to get help for himself, as well as to send reinforcements back to the others.

Jeb stood rubbing his whiskery chin with the back of a hand, considering. It was senseless to hope that they could withstand the full strength Sperling could throw against them, however bitter the thought of giving up. He contemplated mounting and intercepting the departing man but knew it could gain him nothing beyond the purchase of a little time.

He crept to the other corner of the building and took a cautious look at the shack. There was little chance that he could cross to it without drawing fire, some of which might come from his nester friends if they failed to recognize him in the darkness. Even as he weighed this he heard the beat of massed hoofs and repressed a groan. It was too late to join Jorgan and Teebo and try to get out of there. They had to fight it out where they were.

It dawned on him that the hoof drum came from the south, and he slid back into the barn and waited inside

112

the front door, puzzled and tense. Then half a dozen horsemen materialized from the night exactly as the first attackers had done. They came up to where the Dollarmark mounts had been left and, to his surprise, hazed them off at a gallop.

A Dollarmark voice rang out from the creek brush. "Them's nesters, boys! They's chased off our horses!"

Jeb ran into the open, waving his hat and pointing an arm toward the creek. He recognized Trace Getty and Buff Corey in the lead and understanding came. They had seen the burning Hooker buildings from their position on the east desert. The nesters gathered his meaning and, still mounted, charged on toward the creek.

Jorgan and Teebo had come outside, yelling excitedly, but the Sperling men were already on the run. The upset had confronted the raiders with the unbridled fury of men who, that night, had suffered the final outrage. The Sperling men crossed the creek, shooting wildly, then in concert they realized the hopelessness of their predicament, for they were not only set afoot, they were badly outnumbered. One by one the five of them threw down their guns and surrendered.

They were marched back to the yard between the house and barn, where Getty said furiously, "I've got plenty of rope, boys, and they've asked for it!"

Corey's voice rapped out. "Cut that out, Trace. I lost my buildings, but you ain't, so far. There's somethin' lower than burnin' a man out, and that's lynchin'. We'll turn these huckleberries over to the law."

For a moment the thing hung on a precarious balance, for even Corey's sons seemed to share Getty's raging desire. Surprisingly, it was Jimmy Hooker, who also had lost his buildings, who settled it. "Buff's right. There's one thing Hock Sperling can't destroy, and that's the decency in a man. I don't reckon we ought to do that for him voluntarily."

Getty swung toward Jeb. "What the blazes went on here? You were gonna keep 'em out of the Gap, and there's Dollarmark steers all over!"

Jeb felt his back hair raise, but Jorgan cut in placatingly. "Simmer down, Trace. Sperling pulled a whizzer so fast we were helpless. Made his new gather on the plateau, shoved the stuff onto the mountain and let the wind drift it down on us. We wouldn't of saved your buildings, even, if Jeb hadn't had brains enough to check and stumble onto what they were up to."

Getty was taking the defeat the hardest of any of them although, on the surface, he had no more, if as much, at stake. His secret frustration had shaken him, Jeb thought, and still would not let go.

"Fine chance we got now!" he blazed.

Quietly, Jeb said, "I don't see it that way, Getty."

"Why not?"

"We've got Sperling's toughest gun hands right here. I hit another that won't be much use to him a while. He gave himself a lot of work when he cleaned off the plateau to steal his march. He's got to restock it from that side, on top of holdin' the mesa. He's gonna be shorthanded, himself, for a change."

Getty looked skeptical but he was listening. "So?"

"I reckon we didn't notice somethin' in all the excitement. The wind's dyin' down."

"Why," said Corey, "I'll be blamed if it aint."

Turning to look at him, Jeb said, "I hope that means our stuff can hold out a few days more."

"Why, it can," Corey said in rising excitement. "Providin' we gather and herd it a little."

"Then we're not licked yet."

"Mebbe not," Getty said in a gusty voice. "Let 'em burn my shack, too. What counts is bringin' that old coot to his knees, and we won't waste time defendin' this place."

"I don't think he'll burn you out," Jeb said, "with five of his men in jail charged with arson. And we'd best get out of here before more show up and take 'em away from us."

Chapter 15

THEY MADE UP a pack of all the food, blankets, matches, camp equipment and ammunition Getty had in the house.

Meanwhile Matt and Mark Corey rode into the Gap for the canvas that had been used to make shelters. Afterward they all struck out to the east, taking the prisoners with them on the recaught Dollarmark horses. When they were well away from Muleshoe, the Corey brothers held the prisoners while the others drew apart to make plans.

The Coreys, Hooker and Teebo would take the pack out to where the cattle were, it was decided, and set up a temporary camp. Jeb, Getty and Jorgan would escort the prisoners to Broken Rock, going over Dogleg well to the north and thus skirting Sperling's roaming men. Then they separated, each group wanting to get as far from Muleshoe as possible before daylight, which was not far off.

The warming weather was a dispensation from Providence, and riding was no longer uncomfortable. Jeb rode with a nester on either side and the thoroughly disheartened Sperling men ahead, and he reflected that Sperling was going to be mystified about his vanished gunhands until he learned what had happened. Arson by night and the armed assault on Getty's place were serious matters, Sperling's first overt crimes. The sentiment in the country, so Getty and the nesters believed, ran against the old time range holders and in favor of the little people. If true, the proud old man was in serious trouble even if he tried to disclaim responsibility for his men's activities.

They were on Dogleg Mountain when dawn split across the sky behind him, and even at that elevation the temperature was not uncomfortable. An hour later they came down on the plateau, angling toward the river. This put them well north of Sperling's operations, and shortly after noon they rode unmolested into Broken Rock.

The Sperling hands, though imports of the last year, had made themselves known in the town and not too favorably. Their passage along the street under nester guard kicked up excitement that soon spread everywhere. By the time the grim-featured squad reached the jail, which stood a block back from the main thoroughfare, townsters in growing numbers were moving in tow.

Broady Smith, the marshal, came out of his cubby hole office. A bewildered uneasiness rose on his thin face when he recognized the men who had pulled up before his door. Like the growing gallery, he knew about the range feud in the basin, but it was outside his bailiwick and a problem a little large for a town peace officer.

"What's this?" he said in a voice lifted by his sudden tension.

"Prisoners for you to hold," Getty said gustily, "till the sheriff can pick 'em up. We're wirin' him."

Smith blinked his eyes. "What's the charge?"

"They burned out Buff Corey and Jimmy Hooker, last night, and shot up my place tryin' to burn out me."

The marshal had no taste for it, even though custom required him to co-operate in county and state cases. Dollarmark was a big, rough outfit and might decide it did not want its men locked up in his jail. "I hardly got room—" he began.

"They don't need room," Getty snapped. "You gonna lock 'em up or ain't you?"

Smith looked at the crowd and saw that most of it wanted to know the same thing. "All right," he said resignedly. "Fetch 'em in."

Once the hard cases were under lock and key, Jeb left it to Getty and Jorgan to wire the county sheriff at Elko and headed for the mercantile where he had equipped himself when he first reached the country. Somebody came thumping along to catch up with him, and when he looked back he saw Buck Gillidge.

"Howdy, Buck," Jeb said. "How's Cash?"

"Fine as of last night." There was a grim set to the old man's face and a glint of temper in his faded eyes. "So Hock finally went too far."

"Well, he gave us our first real legal complaint."

"I wonder if that old cuss knows he's about lost his last friend," Gillidge said explosively. "What in tarnation's he after? Who's gonna look on him as a big man, anymore, even if he builds his ranch bigger'n ever? I wonder if he ever thought of that."

"This town on our side, Buck?" Jeb asked.

"Most of 'em are."

Jeb had a reason for the question. There were some purchases he wanted to make that, a few years ago, no merchant in town would have dared sell to Hock Sperling's enemies. They had reached the store and he nodded to Gillidge and turned through the double doors. A man in a black apron and heavy leather cuffs stood idling behind a counter, the one who had waited on him before. He nodded his head.

"Howdy, Pelton. What can I do for you?" He seemed friendly.

"Got any dynamite?"

The man's eyes bulged. "Sure. There's lots of mining north and west of here."

"That's what I heard. If I bought a little supply, could I depend on it not being noised around?"

The storekeeper pulled a cigar from his vest pocket, bit off the tip and spat it out. "If you mean word not bein' sent to Hock Sperling on the gallop," he said presently, "you could."

"That's what I mean. Have you got a blasting machine, wire and electric caps?"

"We carry the full line. But look here—you know how to use that stuff?"

"I spent the last five years around mining camps. Six months of that I put in underground. As to the question you haven't asked yet—we don't aim to hurt anybody besides ourselves."

The man looked relieved. "All right, but we keep the stuff in a dugout outside of town."

"That's fine. We've got some extra horses, and I'll see if I can rent some pack saddles at the town corral."

Jeb added ammunition and more food to his order, paid for it with his own money, and arranged for it all to be picked up at the store's powder magazine on the edge of town. The corral man refused to rent him pack saddles but announced that he would loan them readily. On the street two other men stopped Jeb, partly from curiosity but also to express their support. This was heartening, but Jeb doubted that Hock Sperling would care a hoot for the opinion of men he considered small potatoes and intruders in his private domain.

Getty and Jorgan had already gone to Anita's place to see Cash, Jeb found when he reached there. They were in the room where Cash lay propped in bed, looking much better than he did the last time Jeb was there.

The wounded man's face broke in a grin when he saw his partner come in.

"Howdy, Jeb," he said heartily. "They say you been holdin' up your and my end both."

"To the extent," Jeb said, "that anybody with more sense than we've got would admit they were licked."

"I got a picture of you admittin' that."

"How you feelin'?" Jeb said, embarrassed.

"Pretty good, but Doc says I'll be here a while."

"With two pretty girls around, you're complainin' about that?"

"Not that, but I keep thinkin' I ought to be helpin' out."

They visited a while, and Jeb found himself watching the door in hope that Anita would put in an appearance. When she did not, he professed a need for a drink of water and went back to the kitchen. Penny was there by herself. She looked worn, but there was a maturity in her pretty face that had not been there before.

She said, "Hello, Jeb," and her voice was tired.

"Howdy, Penny. From the looks of my partner, he couldn't have picked a better nurse."

"He's easy to take care of." She smiled ruefully. "No, he isn't. He's cross and stubborn and ornery, but I like taking care of him. I hear things have gone from bad to worse, Jeb."

"Yes, and they'll get worse yet before they're better. What happened to Anita?"

"She's out in her shop. Why don't you go say hello?"

"I guess not. She sort of took to not liking me plenty."

Penny nodded. "I know. She hasn't said anything, but I know she's troubled, and Cash told me why it is. Are you sure you're right, Jeb?"

"What I feel don't matter. It's what happens that'll count."

"Well, it wouldn't hurt you to say hello to her."

Jeb guessed that was right and went out across the back yard. The door of Anita's pottery shop stood open. He understood why it had been left that way when he stepped inside, for the interior was uncomfortably warm. Anita was down by the kiln and had her back turned to him. The heavy firebrick door of the kiln had been removed and she was bent forward, fishing inside. She wore a housedress now instead of her clay-splattered shirt and Levis. He stood still for a moment, thinking what a pretty figure she made there in her intentness, and a pain in his heart told him she still meant more to him than any other living person.

He moved forward just as she brought from the kiln a fat-bellied bottle and turned with it, her features kindled in a pleasure directed entirely at the piece. He noticed that she had on asbestos gloves. Then she saw him and said, "Oh!" on a sharp breath.

"Now, don't drop the thing," he said. "I done all the damage to your handiwork I want, already. Say, that's a pretty green."

"Isn't it?" she said and could not repress her enthusiasm. "I tried a new glaze. I've got some other new ones in here."

She put down the piece and turned back to the kiln. He remembered how, the other time he was here, she had so completely forgotten everything but what she was doing. She had done it again, and it was pleasant, even if it was only for a moment that they could forget the barrier that had risen between them. She brought other things out of the kiln, paying him no attention. He started to pick up a bowl for a closer look and let go of it gingerly.

"They're still hot," Anita murmured. "Twelve hours ago they were redhot."

"They get that hot?" he said, surprised.

"And stay so for eight or ten hours."

"What do you burn to get that kind of temperature?"

"Charcoal that I get from some burners who make it for mine smelters. The fire's built in that furnace at the bottom, and the heat wraps up around the chamber. Takes time to mature the pieces."

"Seems I read somewhere that art was long."

"And time fleeting."

"Am I buttin' in?"

She sobered, her cheeks coloring. "You're a touchy, suspicious man, Jeb Pelton. I was completing your quotation. I told the boys I'd only be a minute. But the kiln was ready to open, and I'm always dying with curiosity about what I'll find inside. It's tricky, you see. Things hardly ever turn out the way you expect. Sometimes much better and sometimes—ugh."

They walked together to the house, the moment's illusion gone, life's dreary realities restored. Jeb hurried Getty and Jorgan off because they still had to pack up and make the long trip back to the new camp on the desert east of Muleshoe. The prisoners' horses had been left at the corral, and the men replaced the riding saddles with aparejos the corral man loaned them. They went out to the powder magazine outside of town to load the supplies. Around four o'clock they crossed the river bridge and started home, following the roundabout trail they had used coming in.

"I hope a horse don't stumble," Jorgan grumbled, "and blow us sky high."

Jeb laughed. "The stuff don't go off that easy."

"Well, you're welcome to the job of planting it where it'll do us the most good."

The horses were tired, and it was around midnight when they reached camp. The men there had put in the day rounding up cattle, and most of the stuff was accounted for and in fair shape considering the abuse it had taken. The new arrivals ate a long delayed meal, and since everybody was dead tired they all turned in. Eager as they were to take action against Hock Sperling, they had agreed that it would be wise to let him grow complacent before they did so.

The next morning Jeb rode out with Buff Corey to where the displaced cattle were being loosely held. They were now well north of the area into which Dollarmark had scattered them, and were feeding on the white sage that had sent up its tender, nutritious winter sprouts. Water was the main problem, for what there was of it was so scattered it wore the cattle down to find it. Above that hung the danger of a disastrous change of weather at any time.

Afterward they circled and rode onto Dogleg Mountain for a look at the mesa. Dollarmark seemed to have made Getty's place its headquarters on this side. Two or three men were there, and others patrolled the desert side of the mesa in pairs.

120

The rest of the day passed quietly, and the men got as much rest as they could. They ate supper, and shortly after dark Jeb and Getty checked their sixguns, filled the empty loops in their shell belts and mounted fresh horses.

"Good luck, boys," Corey said soberly. "We'll keep our fingers crossed."

Getty had been in high spirits all day, and he laughed. "Just you boys be ready to go into action when we call on you. Don't worry about me and Jeb."

"Well, I am worried," Corey said defiantly. "Plenty."

Jeb did not share Getty's buoyant optimism about the night's venture himself, and the man nettled him. They rode out quietly, cutting a long slant to the southwest that let them circle back to the West Fork pass without too much danger of bumping into a Sperling rider. This precaution took them a couple of extra hours, but they were in no hurry and spared their horses. They climbed to the pass and crossed over to the basin side. The stars came out in a brighter intensity than Jeb liked.

Getty mentioned and dismissed that. "Look, the one thing they ain't lookin' for is a couple of us showin' up right in their own headquarters."

"I hope not," Jeb said.

They found a notch that let them off the rim, then descended onto the basin floor. From there on Jeb was on unfamiliar ground, but Getty knew the way, and they rode steadily onward. Presently they raised the dim lights of Dollarmark, off to the northwest, and reined in.

Getty reached for his tobacco, and because it could be dangerous to smoke there, Jeb was reminded strongly of this man's heavy smoking under tension, a characteristic he believed marked the murderer of his brother. But Getty, himself, reconsidered and put the makings back in his pocket, sighing.

"Well, I guess we go in," he said, "and figure our moves as they come. Hock's been workin' the guts outta his men the past few days. There won't be any skylarkin' at night. All them that's still on this side of the mountain will hit their soogans pretty soon. Sperling's the only one sleepin' in the big house, since Penny quit him. The cook'll be in his shack, the rest in the bunkhouse."

121

They had been over that before, and Jeb wondered if Getty was trying to keep up his nerve by considering the few advantages they would have against terrific odds.

"They've kept up plenty of night horses since they started trouble with us," Getty went on. "We don't need to worry about mounts. The trick's to get to that bunkhouse without settin' off an alarm."

"You want to try that or keep a lookout for Sperling and the cook?"

"Which do you want?"

"Neither one very bad. But I'll take the bunkhouse."

"It's yours."

Chapter 16

A HALF HOUR LATER they left their horses in the wash of the South Fork which, at its juncture with Sperling Creek, bordered two sides of Dollarmark headquarters. The brush of the streams gave them an ample screen and let them move to the edge of the sprawling ranch-yard without having to expose themselves unduly.

When they came into full view of the huddled buildings, Getty let out another of his keyed-up sighs. The big house was dark, as was the cookshack. The windows of the large bunkhouse still showed the mealy yellow of lamplight, and now and then a man's distorted shadow slid across one of the dingy panes. Getty reached for his tobacco, let out another sigh, and brought his hand down empty.

"Not yet," Jeb whispered when Getty stirred restlessly. "Let 'em get settled down."

Another ten minutes passed while Jeb continued to study the yard that lay in dim relief in the shine of the stars. Four buildings formed a roomy, irregular square, of which the elongated dwelling was the south side. Directly across was the cookhouse with its dining room and cook's quarters. On the east Hock Sperling's little office building stood in the foreground, while at a distance behind it ran the barns and corrals. The bunk-house was on the west side, a drab, barracks-like structure not intended for as large a crew as it had held for the past year.

Yet it would not be crowded tonight. Five of Sperling's men were in jail at Broken Rock, eight or ten more were on the mesa to protect the cattle there. That made it likely that there were no more than ten or twelve men bedded down in there. Certainly they were enough, Jeb reflected, more than he had a right to hope to handle successfully.

"Blazes, let's go!" Getty muttered. "I'm getting the willies!"

"All right. You first, and it seems to me your best position is over by Sperling's office. You can see the house and cookshack and cover me, too, from there."

"I had the same notion."

"I'll give you five minutes. If it blows up, make for our horses. We can't take on that many men."

Now that he was moving, Getty's excitement came through in a chuckle. He slid off to the left to circle behind the bunkhouse and cookshack. As the night swallowed him, Jeb reflected on the fact that he was entrusting his life to an unstable, wholly unknown character who undoubtedly hated him. Yet he was persuaded that Getty wanted Sperling at his mercy. This was the one and only chance to gain that end, so he was pretty apt to cooperate for tonight.

Jeb gauged the time he had allowed Getty to get in place. Drawing a deep breath, he moved forward to the back corner of the bunkhouse, his gun fisted, each step placed with care. A few seconds later he gained the front corner, took a keen, screening look over the deserted yard, then turned and moved down the front of the building to the door. For a moment he listened there, hearing no snoring but no talking, either. He turned the knob carefully and began to inch the door inward. He stepped in and shut the panel behind him so as not to highlight his shape.

A man turned over, and for a moment Jeb's heart twitched like a wounded pigeon in his chest. The fellow settled down, and Jeb waited a while, letting his eyes adjust to this deeper darkness. The beds ran out on either side of him, he saw. Some were double springs resting on blocks, and camp cots had been set up to accommodate the extra men. A lot of them were empty now. He wanted to be able to see all the men, even at the risk of trapping himself, and moved toward the end of the room on his right, which had no openings.

He held his breath through ten cautious steps, came to the wall and put his back to it. His voice punched holes in the silence.

"Set up with your hands high, boys! The first one to get reckless gets shot!"

The strangeness of the command coming from a blank wall helped him. None of them had sunken very deep into sleep as yet, and the brittle voice snapped them alert. But they all looked toward the door, then at the windows. He let them find him, one by one. When they did and saw his gun they obeyed, bending their bodies upright in the beds with their arms straight up.

One of the closer ones blurted, "Pelton! What in—!"

"That's right," Jeb said, "and I've got help outside. You, there by the table. Get up real careful and light the lamp."

The fellow obeyed with alacrity, then stood by the table in his day shirt and drooping drawers. The better light let Jeb watch them more closely. But Sperling's toughest hands were in jail, and he had sent his next best to Muleshoe Mesa apparently. Nobody here looked eager to start a ruckus.

Jeb waited. Then he spoke quietly. "Get up one at a time, starting at the far end. Don't let your arms down."

"What're you up to this time, Pelton?" a man said worriedly.

"Do what I told you."

They did it, swinging their legs out of bed and shoving to a stand one by one, eleven all told. He made them form a file in the center of the room. Not until then was he sure they were all beyond reach of a gun.

"One at a time again," Jeb rapped out. "Pick up your duds and get dressed. If I see a man's hand close to a gun, that man get's dropped."

Sweat had cracked through his skin and his knees felt

weak. He watched the Sperling punchers dress and move hastily back into line. If they started anything, he could shoot them to pieces before one of them could accomplish a thing.

Abruptly Getty's voice rang out, "Come out of there, Sperling! And don't think I wouldn't like to kill you!"

Jeb's pulse made a thready run. The old man must have seen the bunkhouse light come on again and grown puzzled by the activity inside. The punchers stirred, muttering, but the lack of gunshots told them that Getty was in command, out there, and they subsided. Maybe Getty had been forced to yell that way, instead of slipping up on Sperling, but he must have aroused the cook in his quarters.

"Outside, boys!" Jeb ordered. "If anybody gets funny when he's outta my sight, I'll kill somebody I *can* see."

They went through the door, and he followed closely, then Getty yelled encouragingly from closer at hand. "It's all right, Jeb! I got 'em covered!"

Jeb followed the last man out and saw that Getty had somehow secured a double-barreled shotgun. Its threat was enough to keep the Dollarmark outfit quiet, including Sperling.

Getty laughed. "The old boy don't keep his office locked, Jeb. So I paid a visit to his gun rack in there. Both barrels're loaded, and I sure wish somebody'd make me prove it."

Jeb joined him, annoyed by Getty's almost irresponsible excitement. The Dollarmark men were lined along the front of the bunkhouse, and Hock Sperling stood there in his shirt sleeves, his beady old eyes glittering in the starshine.

"Sperling," Jeb said, "we don't want to hurt anybody. But we sure will if one of you's senseless enough to start trouble. Each of these men is gonna saddle himself a horse. If one of 'em gets foxy, you're gonna die. They don't look very bright. So maybe you better give 'em your judgment of whether I mean it."

Sperling shifted his feet, then looked at his men. "Nothing's past this scum," he growled. "Saddle yourselves horses and don't make trouble." He was stunned,

125

mystified, but too arrogantly proud to demand an explanation.

The men had seen too much come from the nesters to take chances with them now. They moved toward the horse corral, thoroughly cowed by the shotgun in Getty's hands and his ill-concealed desire to use it. If he possessed the means to interfere, the cook must have lacked the courage, for nothing developed from him. The Dollarmark men caught and saddled horses and brought them back to the yard. Sperling stood helplessly by, now and then shaken by outrage but too realistic to rebel.

Jeb turned the remaining horses out of the corral and gave them a running start across the big pasture, then brought up his and Getty's mounts.

"Sperling," Getty said when they were ready to move out, "I'd admire to take you along. But Jeb says you're too old to live through what your cowhands have got coming. So you can set here feelin' how it is without an army of gunslingers to back your hand."

Dismay got the best of Sperling, and he gasped, "What are you up to?"

"You'll have plenty of time to puzzle on it, old man."

At Jeb's clipped order the Dollarmark hands moved out. Getty held onto the lethal scattergun he had appropriated. They headed southeast toward Sapphire Mountain and the West Fork pass. An hour later they threaded the pass and not long after midnight came down on the edge of Muleshoe Mesa.

"Bear south!" Jeb called ahead.

"Where you takin' us?" a man shouted back.

"Keep ridin', buck," Getty answered, "and you'll learn."

Jeb rode with a jumpy alertness now, and even Getty was sobered. The Sperling line riders were covering this end of the mesa, too, and unless they were eluded in the darkness they could make serious trouble. But an hour passed, then another, and then they were pretty far south for that to happen. Thereupon the cavalcade turned east toward the sink that lay out there in its sterile surroundings. The stolidly riding prisoners began to look about apprehensively but, disarmed, they were impotent. At long last the procession reached the cuesta on the west side of the marshes, and the escorts called a halt.

"Get down from the horses," Jeb told them.

"You gonna massacree us?" a puncher asked in a trembling voice.

"Dismount. Everybody."

They did not object enough to risk life and limb in a dispute. When they had obeyed, Jeb told them to move well away from the horses.

"All right," he said finally. "If you start right now and don't get too many blisters to walk any farther, you might get back to Dollarmark tonight. But I'd swing wide of Muleshoe, if I was you. Your friends won't be in charge of it much longer."

"You ain't gonna set us afoot in this country!" one of them cried in alarm.

"From the crew Dollarmark had when it brought our steers down here to die," Jeb said coldly, "you fellows must've been along. I don't expect you quibbled about that. You've still got your strength and you can walk faster and farther than a steer. So get at it."

They protested and some of them swore bitterly but they started out. Jeb and Getty tied their horses in two strings and, leading them, headed for the nester camp farther north.

The late, autumn dawn was still a couple of hours away when they rode up to the campfire. The approach of so many horses had alerted the men there, and they were on their feet and waiting.

"You pulled it off," Jorgan said incredulously. "I never dared to expect it."

"Where you think we got these Dollarmark cayuses?" Getty said, with his exuberant laugh. "Hock Sperling's afoot in his big pasture, too, tryin' to catch somethin' to ride. The cowpokes we dumped at the sink ain't gonna be in shape to loan him no help, either. And the eight or ten on Muleshoe don't have any idea of what went on."

"We've still got to get Sperling's herd off the mesa," Jeb pointed out.

"We can do that, too, now that they're whittled down to our size."

Buff Corey had poured coffee and the others had taken charge of the horses. Jeb took a sip of the warming brew. "Getty knows the layout at his place like his own

127

hand. With a couple of others, he ought to be able to take it over again. If so, he can lock up whoever he catches there and start working the cattle on that end toward the Gap. The rest of us can start on this end and work north. Did you get a look at their line riders, Buff?"

"Yeah," Corey answered. "There's six, ridin' in couples. They patrol along the east edge of the mesa, and that's all."

Jeb nodded. "They figure trouble'll come from this direction. With luck, we can get a lot of stuff movin' on the other side of 'em before they catch on. When they do, there'll only be two of 'em to handle at a time. That sort of lonesomeness kind of takes the steam out of hired gunhands. They like to work in packs."

Jorgan's square Swedish face was lighted by a grin. "We gotta show, boys, which was more than I could see when you two fellers set out tonight. The rest of us owe you plenty for that. This is the first time we've went up against somebody our own size. Let's see how we do with it."

"How about ridin' them Dollarmark horses?" Teebo asked. "It'll be light before we've hardly got started. In the distance a man'll recognize a cayuse he knows before he does the rider."

"That's the ticket," Getty agreed.

They were soon mounted on the captured horses and divided into two parties. Taking Jorgan and Teebo with him, Getty struck off to the northwest, and Jeb slanted southwest with the four Coreys and Hooker. The morning star was out by the time they reached the south tip of the mesa, warning that daylight was but an hour or so off.

Jeb chose the east line to ride northward, leaving the cattle moving in charge of Buff Corey. Fortunately, the country was open so that, although they were bound to miss some stuff, the bulk of it could be located and started moving without much trouble. Once such a movement was going, it would snowball automatically as long as there were riders in the rear doing a little shoving.

128

Chapter 17

A STRANGE SERENITY lay on Muleshoe, and the night seemed to deepen as the stars faded out. There was no wind and, after the frigid blow of the last two days, the air seemed comfortable and pleasant. In the predawn obscurity Jeb could see nothing of the men with him, and nothing had yet presented itself due ahead on the line the Dollarmark punchers were patrolling.

He found himself thinking of many things: the job he had left at Randsburg expecting to be gone only a week or two, the unexpected embroilment here that had changed the course of his life, the friends he had made and the enemies, and, above all, the girl who had become the center of his deepest feelings and thoughts. If this last onslaught against Sperling paid off, the showdown with Trace Getty would follow immediately. No matter how that turned out, Jeb reflected, the breach between him and Anita would become permanent.

He came alert when, in the far foreground, he discerned the vague, small shapes of riders. It was still too dark for them to be fooled by the Dollarmark horse he straddled and, after a moment's thought, he swung the horse to the right and rode off in that direction for some distance. He halted presently and remained motionless while he watched the oncomers. They drew slowly nearer, themselves lulled by the night's deep feeling of peace.

When the two horses halted summarily, out there, he knew he had been seen. He did not budge, and their uncertainty drew them on for another hundred yards before they pulled up again. Slowly and deliberately he turned his horse to the east, raised on the stirrups and waved his hat several times as if signalling to confederates off in the dark concealment of the desert. Then he turned back toward them, and they sat unmoving while they tried to figure him out. Abruptly they wheeled their mounts and went driving north. He had gulled them into thinking an attack in force was poised, and they had decided that they could use some help.

He rode swiftly west, and the first nester he came upon proved to be Matt Corey. The smell of dust in the still air told him that they had got a number of Dollarmark steers moving on the long drift north to the Gap. He told Matt about the Sperling riders, adding, "They'll pick up the others and come foggin' back. It'll be getting light by then, and they'll see you fellows. Tell the others to be ready for trouble, too. Meanwhile I'll see if I can mix the cusses up a little more."

"Sure," Matt said, "but don't get yourself killed. Pa says you're the one that's pulled us this far outta the hole. We're gonna need you the rest of the way, too."

Jeb rode on north, keeping well over to the west. Buff Corey had said there were six Sperling men riding line. That was enough to break up the drive if they were allowed to take the offensive. He rode at a thumping gait, not caring that the sound of it might carry to them. Any way he could confuse them would help the nesters.

He reached the wash of the east fork of Mesa Creek just as dawn rent the sky and was only a little way from the site of Jimmy Hooker's burned buildings. Dropping into the wash he turned east, riding beside the stream that bisected the wide, sandy creek bed. In the strengthening light he found the place where the Sperling men had been crossing regularly on their patrols. In all probability the pair he had excited had been by here already, heading north, but they would come back this way with reinforcements. So deciding, Jeb swung out of the saddle, trailed the reins of the Dollarmark horse in a patch of seep grass, then slipped into hiding behind a downed old cottonwood.

He had to wait a long while, but the tired and hungry horse stood there, quietly feeding. At last his keening ears caught the sound they sought, that of rapid mounted travel to the north. His pulses quickened. The sound neared, then they broke over the bank of the wash, as yet cut off from sight of the grazing horse by the trees along the stream, six men—the whole patrol. If he could

130

stop them, the night's work would reach fruition; if he failed it was ruined.

They splashed across the narrow, shallow stream, came out of the nearer trees and halted, mystified. "Say," a man said, his voice loudened by surprise, "that cayuse is out of Baldy's string. What's it doin' way over here?"

"There's somebody's tracks," another commented.

"Hold it."

Jeb had risen from behind the fat old tree trunk, his gun clutched in his fist, his lean face grim. A man let out a squawk and stabbed a hand toward his sixshooter. Jeb's barking gun spat a bullet that knocked the hat from the belligerent man's head.

"That's the last break you get," Jeb's heavy voice rapped out. "Start loosenin' buckles. I want to see every shell belt hit the sand."

The face of the man who had lost his hat was pasty white, and his fear had telegraphed itself to the others. Nobody else felt lucky enough to make the same play, and the gun harnesses came loose and dropped. Jeb let them lay there and walked to the horse that had thrown them off balance and mounted it.

He gave them the flat, frigid impact of his eyes and said, "Start riding. East."

They came out of the wash at the charred remains of Hooker's place. From the look on the faces of the Sperling men, he knew they wondered if they were to be treated with the same callous savagery their side had shown. He failed to relieve their worried minds and kept them riding steadily into the eastern distance, the day now fully born without them. He kept them going at a trot for two hours, then dismounted them, took their horses and started back for the mesa alone.

He slanted toward the north end and, to his relief, came upon Getty, Jorgan and Teebo working cattle along the mesa's eastern edge.

"So you took care of the men at your place," he said.

Getty grinned. "Caught 'em asleep. Yerington, himself, and two others."

"What did you do with 'em?"

"Left 'em hogtied. What you been doin' over east?"

Jeb told them what had happened and that the way was clear to clean the Dollarmark cattle off Muleshoe. "If," he stipulated, "we get it cut by night. That's about all the time we'll have before Dollarmark's back together. Fuller of fight than they've ever been."

There was no elation in the others, for they realized that the tide was bound to set in against them again before long. They went back to work, while Jeb rode south to find Corey's crew. They had the drive on that end going well by then, and he set out to help them. By noon they were even with Corey's burned headquarters, hungry and tired, but they kept going.

In midafternoon Jeb rode north to find that Getty and his helpers had started drifting cattle through the Gap into Sperling Basin. By then the whole central mesa was covered with a thin dust as the bovine invaders drew slowly but surely into a cohesive mass. By late afternoon cattle were moving steadily into the connecting canyon and on out to the basin. What happened to them on that side did not matter; the important thing was to make it impossible for them to come back.

The windup came in the last hours of light. When the final steer had been pushed into the stricture, the nesters let out a wild, whooping yell. They were a grimy looking bunch, by then, and nearly worn out, but there was work yet to be done. Getty and the two men who had helped him that day volunteered to stand guard at the Gap. The others headed out for the desert camp to move in the cattle and supplies there.

They had collected themselves a fair-sized remuda of Dollarmark horses and, when they had cooked a quick meal over a campfire, the others helped Jeb load the packsaddles they had borrowed in Broken Rock. Then they turned their attention to the nester cattle, which had yet to be returned to its rightful range on the mesa, while Jeb started back for the Gap.

He dropped everything but the explosives on the east end of the big canyon to be taken to Getty's place later. He went on into the passage to where Getty and his companions had taken up their old sentry posts on the west end. Getty had already gone home and brought out a posthole digger and a shovel, and they were nearly

132

finished digging a line of holes that stretched across the canyon, just in from the mouth.

"But you can have the rest of the job," Getty said, "and welcome to it."

Jeb had handled enough dynamite to lose his fear, although not his respect for it, and he set to work. Two hours later each of the postholes was mined with a pack of six sticks of dynamite in which was embedded an electric blasting cap. The detonators, in turn, were connected by a long wire with the blasting machine placed deeper in the canyon, beyond the protection of a bend.

"One stroke of the plunger," Teebo said with an admiring look at the machine, "and there's a crater and heap of dirt so big in that canyon Dollarmark couldn't get mountain goats across."

Jeb himself was satisfied, at last, with the grueling day's outcome, but they had only got out of one predicament. Even if the Sperling cattle were kept off the mesa, thereafter, the nester steers would badly overcrowd it. And they were a long way from regaining the range on Dogleg Plateau, which they had to have if they were to survive, themselves.

Getty said, "Well, you three can hold down the fort here. I reckon I'll ride out and lend the boys a hand with our steers."

All through a maddening night and day Hock Sperling had carried with him a growing sense of vulnerability that had in it strong hints of doom. He had learned that day that five of his men were locked up in the Broken Rock jail, to be charged with arson. In the early night, when he saw nearly a dozen more men driven from his headquarters under the guns of a measly pair, he felt that his whole plan was falling apart. Later, he had carried a catch rope into the big pasture and spent hours trying to get horse flesh under him so he could do something. Giving that up, he had returned and lambasted the cook for not breaking up the raid. He had even threatened to make the fifteen mile walk to Head Creek to reach Lot Yerington and horses.

The cook, who was nearly as old as he was, finally let fly.

"Darn it, Hock, quit talkin' like a crazy loon! All I had was my old hoss pistol, and I don't see good enough at night to take on hombres like them two. I'd of got some of our men killed, mebbe you. As for you walkin' to Head Creek, that's ridiculous. Neither of us could hoof it half way there afore we played out. You simmer down before you bust a artery in your head and get a stroke."

"What're they up to?" Sperling demanded.

"They ain't been lettin' me in on their secrets. I allow that, whatever it is, it won't be to your liking. But there's nothin' you can do about it right now, so why don't you hit the hay?"

"Horse sweat," Sperling said and stomped out of the cookshack.

But he had vented a little spleen and pretty soon began to get hold of himself. Pelton and Getty had pulled off a daring thing here, but it had succeeded only because it had been wholly unexpected. There were only nine of the nesters, and they certainly were not going to do much damage to Dollarmark. The big danger was the uncertain weather. He did not have time to seesaw back and forth. The thing had to be settled in his favor, and now.

He went over to the office, got out his bottle and had a stiff drink. Presently he stretched out on the old horsehair couch there, not intending to sleep, but before he knew it he dropped off. He awakened stiff and cold and struck a match to see that it was nearly daylight.

The cook had got up from deep-worn habit, and there was light in his place of business. Sperling went over and got a cup of coffee and lighted a cigar.

Savagely, he said, "Why ain't anybody showed up?"

The cook shrugged and set a plate of flapjacks before him. "Won't do you no good to starve yourself. Eat that."

Sperling shoved the food away.

After daylight he went down to the big pasture gate to see if some of the horses had drifted in, as they did sometimes. None had, and he began to feel that they were against him, too. In all the years he had lived there he had never been caught without horses held up with which to catch more. He had forgotten how far it was between places. But he was far from being as enfeebled as that ornery old cook thought. He started for Head Creek on foot.

It was a long way in his high heeled boots, and he had to stop more and more often to rest. But he had covered the twelve miles to the Gap by noon and had just got there when the first Dollarmark steers came drifting through from the mesa side. Unbelievable as it seemed, he understood then what was going on. When the steers kept coming through in increasing numbers he knew better than to try to make his own way on to the mesa when he did not understand the situation there. Too many men hated him bitterly, now, after the burning of those nester shacks.

It took nearly all afternoon for him to make his way back home. He slouched wearily to his office, pulled off his boots, and got out the whiskey bottle. There was no fire in the stove, but he failed to notice the cold.

It was long after dark when he heard a sound he had wanted to hear so long, but it did not seem to matter now. A horse was coming in. The whiskey bottle was empty by then, but he was not drunk. He failed to get up to see who the newcomer was. Pretty soon the office door swung inward, and in the darkness he did not recognize the shape of the man who stood there.

"Sperling?" a voice said.

"Getty!" Sperling gasped. "What did you come back here for?"

He heard the man's chuckle. "I ain't supposed to be here. You know you're licked, don't you, old man?"

"I ain't any such thing," Sperling growled.

The chuckle became a laugh. "Sperling, your steers're back in the basin, and the Gap's mined from wall to wall. You come anywhere near with a herd, and we'll blow it up. You can't come over Dogleg again with us onto you, unless you want to lose half the steers. We can hold the two high passes with guns. And did you notice something while you were settin' here gnawing on your vitals? It turned a lot colder tonight."

"What'd you do to my men?" Sperling retorted.

"They'll be driftin' in pretty soon. Afoot. That's all

135

that happened to 'em, except Lot Yerington and a couple of others. They're tied up at my place."

"What'd you come here for? To gloat?"

"No," Getty said gently. "To help you out."

"How?"

"I can deliver everything you want in twenty-four hours."

"Ah," Sperling said after a long moment. "How much?"

"Ten thousand. Cash. Cheap, considerin' what you stand to lose."

"What makes you think you can deliver?"

"Them nesters couldn't have got to first base against you without me. You know that."

Sperling snorted. "Jeb Pelton's twice the man you are."

Angrily, Getty said, "All right, without me and Pelton. With us out of the picture, they'd still give up quick."

"Pelton's ready to sell 'em out, too?"

"You don't have to put it that way. I never was on their side. All I ever wanted was to get you where I could make you pay me. Big. You're there now. Let me put your cash in my pants, and I'll take care of Pelton and clear out for good. All you couldn't get from fightin' will be yours just like that."

"I don't think you can handle Pelton," Sperling snapped. "How? By killing him?"

"He's out to get me. More'n he wants to beat you. I don't aim to let him."

"I'll have to get the money from the bank," Sperling said. "Borrow it. Couldn't do that before tomorrow morning."

"Get it," Getty said. "Meanwhile I'll take care of Pelton, which I aim to do, anyway. I'll be in town at noon. Meet me and turn over the money, and I'll take the train for yonder. Back out, and I'll stick with the nesters till you're ruined."

Sperling took another long moment before he said, "All right."

Getty faded from the doorway. Pretty soon his horse moved out.

Sperling sat there a long while afterward, a feeling of deep aversion soaking through his tired body. He had

136

condoned murder, technically he had connived in it. He had done a lot of cruel things, some of them illegal, but he had never gone that far before. But they had forced him to it, the invaders, the disloyal ones and, most of all, the changing times.

She arrived so quietly that he did not hear her come in from the creek road. She must have gone to the lighted cookshack first and learned where he was, for the office door opened again, and he saw a woman's shape, and Penny's voice came to him across the darkness.

"Grandpa?"

"Penny?" He was surprised that his own voice held a quaver.

She went to his desk, and he heard a match strike, then light exploded in the room, blurring his vision. She lifted the chimney from the lamp and touched the match to the wick. She replaced the chimney and turned up the wick.

She said, "What was Trace Getty doing here?"

"Getty? Why, nothing much. You come home?"

She turned, and his eyes were adjusted to the light by then. Perhaps it was because he had not seen her for a while that he was so strongly struck by her resemblance to her mother, his daughter. Young, fresh and so very lovely. He could not read her face too well at the moment, except he knew that she still clung to her unforgiveness.

"Getty wasn't here for a trivial reason, Grandpa. Did he sell out to you?"

"What're you talking about?" he said, but there was so little force in his voice he knew he had set her suspicions.

"So Jeb Pelton was right, all along. Getty's a traitor."

"You come out here to preach?" he demanded.

She shook her head. "Buck Gillidge has been keeping tabs on things out here. He told me they threw your steers off Muleshoe, today. The nesters have fought you to a draw. I came to make one more plea. Give it up before you destroy yourself completely."

"Destory myself? I ask nothing but what's mine, and I'll have it yet."

137

"So you made a deal with Getty. That's the only way you could." She turned toward the door.

"Where you going?" he said uncertainly.

"I think the nesters ought to know about that."

"Don't you—!"

She slipped through the door. In a moment he heard her horse go out of the yard, its hoofs thundering. A sudden clawing fear went through him, not for what she would do but for her safety. If she had seen and recognized Getty as she came in, he had seen and recognized her. Getty knew that by his mere presence here, in this critical hour, he had confirmed the suspicion against him.

Sperling stumped out through the doorway, shouting after her. Only the fading drum of hoofs answered him.

Chapter 18

IT HAD grown notably colder in the four hours since nightfall, and Jeb was thinking of Yerington and his two men who had been left tied up at Getty's place. They had been there that way all day, and he had no desire to inflict unnecessary suffering on them. He was standing a trick at the mouth of the canyon with Jorgan while Teebo warmed himself at a fire deeper in the passage. They still mounted guards in pairs, since there was danger of one of them growing sleepy and careless. They were across the Gap from each other to lessen the danger of being sneaked up on and overcome.

He had decided to go back and get Teebo to relieve him, while he rode to Head Creek and turned the Dollarmark men loose, when the growing beat of hoofs, out in the basin, reached his ears. The sound puzzled him, but there were no nesters on that side of the mountain to worry about. It came on, growing louder, then all at once the staccato punch of gunshots cut through the night. There were three of them, then silence, not even the hoof beat any longer.

"What was that?" Jorgan yelled from his side.

138

"You got me," Jeb called back.

Teebo had heard the shooting, too, for in a few minutes he came hurrying along the canyon. "You reckon that was a decoy to get us to leave here and investigate?" he asked.

"Could be," Jeb said. "It's a cinch none of our boys are out there."

"Well, if Dollarmark's took to killin' each other off," Teebo reflected, "it suits me fine. Let's stay put."

They waited through a cold half hour and, when nothing more developed, their tension eased. Jeb began to think about Yerington and mentioned it.

"Go ahead," Jorgan agreed. "If that shootin' was meant to pull us away from here, we didn't fall for it. Me and Leet can hold the fort while you're gone."

Jeb rode through to the east end of the Gap, where the remaining supplies had been dumped and the Dollarmark horses picketed. He took three of the extra animals with him and rode on toward Head Creek, crossing range that now was empty.

He came in on the benighted buildings at Getty's place, dismounted at the shack and went in. "Who's that?" a strained voice demanded, and he knew that if they were still here they were still bound and helpless.

He struck a match and saw them, three men tied in a sitting position on straight-backed chairs. He frowned when he saw that Getty had tied them up the way he found them, in their shirt sleeves, and he saw a mixture of misery, apprehension and fury on their faces.

"You're a bunch of lowdown savages," Yerington growled. "Lettin' us freeze to death."

"Take it easy."

Jeb did not blame him for his temper but had no wish to commiserate. He lighted the table lamp and regarded them.

"You can't do any good trying to jump me," he said to Yerington. "Even if you overcome me before I shot one of you. Your cattle's off the mesa for keeps. Your crew's scattered and afoot. Accept that and behave, and I'll untie you. Otherwise you can set there the rest of the night."

"All right," Yerington said. "But get these ropes off quick."

Jeb freed them and knew it would be a while before they could even move very well. He kindled a fire in the cookstove, appreciating its growing warmth himself, and put a batch of coffee on to cook. The Dollarmark men were massaging their cramped muscles, stretching and stomping. While there was little fight in them at the moment, he watched them cagily.

The trio soaked up the heat and when the coffee was ready drank it gratefully. Afterward they got into their wraps and took the Dollarmark horses Jeb had brought for that purpose.

"Go over Dogleg," he warned them. "Too many nesters around with more reason to hate your guts than I've got."

They rode off sullenly into the night.

Jeb went back into the shack and put on more coffee, wanting it himself. While waiting for it to cook he rolled and lighted a cigarette, puzzling over the shooting in the basin. He was pouring a cup of coffee when the door opened behind him.

"Howdy, Jeb," Getty said.

Jeb turned, and the man stood there with a gun held firmly in his fist, a cold grin of malice on his face. Getty came on in and closed the door, then stood there with his back to it, savoring the moment.

"I reckon you ain't so surprised."

"I just didn't expect it yet," Jeb said. "So you didn't go to help bring in the steers."

"I don't give a hoot about them steers."

"Made your deal with Sperling? I take it that's where you went."

Getty's glinting eyes narrowed. "You're just smarter'n all get out, ain't you? Too smart for your own good, like Tom was."

"You didn't realize Buck Gillidge also knows your record when you killed Tom, I guess."

"Still playin' it smart," Getty said with a sneer. "Tryin' to get me to admit I did."

"You don't have to admit it. I know you did. You also marked up his grave after you heard I was coming. Call-

140

ing Tom a dirty nester would make me blame Dollar-mark for that and for the killing, which I did. But I never stayed fooled, and you knew almost from the start that you'd have to kill me, too. By getting the big edge on me, like now."

"You've still got your gun. Why don't you reach for it?"

"I'm no fool. But you are, Getty. Your deal with Sperling involved killing me. It had to, for I've horned you out as the nesters' real leader, and you and Sperling know it. Kill me, and he'll let the law hang you instead of paying you off. If there wasn't evidence enough against you, he'd frame you. Think he wants you around to blackmail him the rest of his life?"

"I don't aim to be around."

"He can't trust you for that."

Fear had risen in Getty's eyes, too much of it to come solely from what Jeb had said.

"Ah," Jeb murmured. "You were in the basin just now. Who did you kill there, Getty, that's worryin' you, too? Somebody comin' to warn me? A horse was heading fast for the Gap, then there were some shots, and nobody ridin' all at once. Who was it?"

"Hold it, stand still!"

But he had caught Jeb's edging motion too late. Jeb's hand swept out and hit the lamp, and it went flying across the room. Getty's gun exploded just as Jeb threw himself headlong to the floor. The lamp had gone out even before it hit the wall and shattered. The stove draft still threw a little light into the room. Getty shot again while Jeb clawed for his own gun, and that bullet hit the table leg by Jeb's head. And in the moment of silence that followed the clatter of hoofs reached them.

Getty swung open the door with a choked protest and went through into the night as Jeb shot. The snap shot missed, apparently, for in a moment Getty's horse was driving out.

Jeb sprang to his feet and raced to the door, knowing that his life would not be safe again as long as Getty lived. His own horse stood out there; Getty in his haste had not thought to drive it off. Jeb was hatless and coatless, and after the heat of the shack the deepening outer

141

cold was a shock. He vaulted into the saddle, swung the horse, and went driving in the direction Getty had taken toward Dogleg Mountain, although he had lost sight of the man in the night.

He had scarcely covered a hundred yards when the foreground was rent by exploding guns. He drove on and in a moment saw a horseman riding toward him, waving his hat. Jeb responded in the same wise and when they came together Jeb saw that it was Buck Gillidge.

"He's back there," Gillidge said, a motion of his head indicating the region behind him.

"You got him?"

"He's dead. First man I ever killed, but thank the Lord I done it. He tried to kill Penny."

"Penny?"

Gillidge nodded and explained. He had gone over to Anita's house to see Cash and learned that Penny had gone to the basin to see her grandfather. Worried about her making the ride, part of which would be after dark, Buck had got his horse and followed her. He had reached Dollarmark to find Sperling there helpless for lack of a mount and worried to death for Penny. Buck had hurried on, but too late. He had come upon her dead horse, with her lying there stunned from the spill. He had brought her to and learned that Getty had shot at her twice before he finally killed her horse. Buck had come on to warn Jeb in her place, had heard the shooting at the shack and feared that Jeb was dead until he saw him after intercepting the fleeing killer.

"Glad it was me that got him," Buck concluded. "It would have been a fearful thing to stand between you and Anita all your lives."

"She'll never forgive me, anyhow."

"No?" Buck said. "On what grounds, since you've been proved right? I left Penny where I found her. We best get back to her."

They stopped in the Gap, borrowed Jorgan's saddled horse and went on to where Buck had left Penny. She pronounced herself all right except for bruises and abrasions, and they returned to Dollarmark. Sperling's dispirited crew had begun to slog in from their long hikes from the east desert, all of them having had to by-pass the nester-held mesa and cross the mountain on foot.

The old man did not come out of his office until the three horses stopped in front of it. Then he appeared in the doorway.

"Penny!" he said in a choked voice. "You—you're all right!"

"Yes," she said gently, and got down from the horse. The two men followed her into the office where Sperling stood looking at her, a broken and very old man. Penny spoke again, her voice clearly marked by compassion. "Don't worry about it, Grandpa."

"Tonight," Sperling said huskily, "you warned me I might destroy myself. I didn't see how till I nearly destroyed you. Once I did see—but what's the use? I sound like a licked man tryin' to beg off. What I put in your heart and mind against me will stay there. Nothin' I can do will take it out."

"That depends on what you're going to do. Keep fighting?"

Sperling shuddered. "There'll be charges against me for burnin' out the nesters, maybe for conniving in a murder attempt. I'll plead guilty and hope that's the end of it."

"Sperling," Jeb said, "there'll be no charge of attempted murder. Restore those destroyed buildings and give up Dogleg Plateau, and there'll be no arson charge, either. You can put those extra steers of yours on a hay ranch down the river till they're fat enough to sell."

"And get rid of them mad dogs workin' for you," Buck Gillidge added. "And open your ornery mind to the fact that a new day's come."

Sperling looked at them somberly. "I'm not beggin' off."

"Of course not," Penny said in her gentle way, "but nobody wants to make bad matters worse. Will you do what they say?"

Sperling nodded, then his eyes turned spunky as he looked at Gillidge. "I'm not so sure a new day's come, Buck. New conditions, yes. But there's still real men around even if some have turned nester. I was slow to see it, that's all."

143

Smiling, Penny turned to the other two men. "I'll stay here tonight. Will you go in and tell Cash so he won't worry? You, too, Jeb. You're not the one who hurt Anita. The one who did is dead."

"She's talkin' gospel, son," Gillidge said.

Jeb pulled in a deep breath and knew that they spoke the truth. "You'll have to hustle to keep up with me, Buck," he said.

THE END